OUT OF AZTLAN

V. CASTRO

Creature Publishing
Brooklyn, NY

This is a work of fiction. Names, characters, places, and incidents either are the products of the author's imagination or are used fictitiously. Any resemblance to actual persons, living or dead, events, or locales is entirely coincidental.

ISBN 978-1-951971-09-0
LCCN 2022947029

Cover design by Luísa Dias
Spine illustration by Rachel Kelli

CREATUREHORROR.COM
@creaturelit
@creaturepublishing

Dedicated to the ancestors and spirits for this life

CONTENTS

Aztlan

I wandered for years in and out of different skins, colors of lipsticks, shoes, and beds. But still I could not find the path that led to Aztlan. No one could tell me where to start. I wondered where my yellow brick road was. Finally, beneath a full moon as I fell to my knees and my head hung towards hell, I realized something. I am Aztlan. This is where it exists. It follows me everywhere I go. It is in the brown skin that I cannot change, the color red that looks best on me, and it doesn't matter if I wear shoes or sleep beneath the stars. There is no Aztlan without me, and I am not me without the trail of bodies in my wake that lead back to the birthplace of who I really am.

And we all have our own Aztlan. We just need to allow ourselves to be led back.

TEMPLO MAYOR

The world began to unlock its doors and open its windows. Signs of life sparked globally with Lazarus quickness. We called it the resurrection of humanity. The heaviness of the past five years rolled away. Everyone busied themselves to reclaim their lives. Many struggled with the economic fallout that had devastated most of the world. Fortunately, I made it through. The Quarantine atrophied my mind and will to the point that I prayed for this world to be cleansed, that something or someone would hear my pleas for change. Could we start over with the knowledge of our past mistakes? Then I would pass out in a deep sleep on my sofa or bed in complete isolation. Sometimes I chatted to family and friends; however, the waves of energy blackouts often left us alone in the dark of the unknown.

Once we could freely move again, I booked a trip to see my family in Texas who I had not seen in five long years, followed by a vacation for myself in Mexico. To stimulate public spending, flights were cheap. Hotels—the ones that survived—splashed grand deals to lure people, at least those who could afford it. All of my savings I poured into living again. Three whole weeks of hearing and seeing other people. Perhaps I would meet someone. How long had it been? My itinerary began in Guadalajara followed by Veracruz, the pyramids on the Yucatan peninsula, and finally Mexico City. Most of my time would be spent there as I wanted the sounds of life to fill my head. Sirens, shouting, laughter, curses, the aroma of street food, live music. I wanted it all. A fresh start. My own resurrection. Of course, many of my friends wondered if it was a good idea for a single woman to be traveling alone. It did make me pause, but fear and anxiety were at an all-time high for everyone.

It was my last day in Mexico City and I only had one place left to see: Templo Mayor, a grand structure built by my ancestors to declare their ingenuity and celebrate the blood that appeased the Gods. When the temple stood in its time of glory, skulls of the conquered and pious decorated wooden stakes for all to see upon arrival. This was a monument intended to awe and instill fear, dedicated to sacrifice with the victims buried beneath. Today only ruins remain, a headstone to a vanquished civilization, with its people absorbed by the ground or dispersed like seeds blown by a strong wind. I am part of that history. My body pumps Mestiza blood. Since I was a child, I had a deep desire to immerse myself in a culture I knew but didn't fully understand. Fate intervened and everyone's big plans came to an abrupt halt for five years and six months.

Before the pestilence, I visited the catacombs in Paris which are just as macabre as this place; however, I did not pre-book a tour and had to wait in a miserable cold drizzle for an hour. When I had the chance to finally descend the staircase leading to the portion of the catacombs open to visitors, I had to push past other tourists to read the well-lit signs telling us the history. It was a unique experience but too many people to take your time. I heard from a friend it was the same for the catacombs in Rome if you visit during peak travel periods. This time I arranged for a private archaeological tour with a small group. Perhaps we could spend a few evenings together if we got along. Some of my closest friends were dead. They'd left a place in my heart that ached night and day considering I did not have the chance to say goodbye. When did the simple things in life become a luxury?

I met a man named Gregory who was a PhD student from UT Austin working on opening unsealed chambers of the temple. Not a soul had set foot inside Templo Mayor since something extraordinary had been found in a new chamber. And not just any chamber. Apparently, there were ancient vestiges of Lake Texcoco. This lake was drained to make space for the city after the Mexica travelled from their supposed home, Aztlan. What would the marshes tell us? Preserved bodies? Artwork? I had to see and smell these ancient waters if I could. With nothing else to occupy my time, I read about it day and night. My imagination ventured to the wild unknown, wondering what lay in wait beneath the temple. The leader of the expedition sanctioned these little tours to provide Gregory with extra cash during his stay. Big discoveries burn through grant money faster than a match thrown in water. And there was not much money circulating with inflation having turned to wildfire.

As I waited for Gregory, I scanned the blackened remnants of the temple which sits in the center of a busy city. This area is called the zocalo. Stone serpents and skulls grimaced as shadows from the waning daylight crossed their faces. I shuddered, imagining what it would have felt like to be led up the great, brightly-painted stairs to be gutted and consumed, or if I was a priest knowing so little of the natural world, thinking blood was the answer to the world's problems? What would they have done in the face of these past five years?

"You made it."

Gregory stood with the setting sun to his back, his strawberry blonde hair highlighting his soft brown eyes. He was better looking in person than the photos on the website offering his services. I wondered what his touch would feel like. A naked body, any body, on mine would be a welcome relief until the right one arrived. Two industries that had boomed during the pestilence were online streaming of amateur porn and sex toys. Some of the single folks like myself lived in desperation to be fucked. Now that humans were mixing again, the online dating scene had taken over. Six different pictures to capture various aspects of who you are at your best with the hopes of finding a match.

"You won't believe it, but the others cancelled. Too much partying last night. It's just us. Hope that's okay."

He looked so good I didn't care that I would be alone with this stranger. I didn't want to be alone anymore, or afraid. My phone was fully charged, and I felt comfortable in this city, more at home than any other place I had visited. And I wanted to see the chamber which led to Lake Texcoco. I found it curious that he was the only one offering such an off-the-grid tour, but every city had some element of that.

We would enter the archaeological site through the cathedral not far from where we stood. The church is also a magnificent sight to see. It, too, is a monument to sacrifice and blood, trying to explain what is unknown. Inside you will find the preserved heart of a saint. Christ did tell the disciples to drink his blood. Priests self-flagellated until their backs ripped open. It is not lost on me that the pagan beliefs came first.

"You are in for a real treat." He flashed me a charming smile.

I had to return a little flirtation. "Really? What is that? I want to see what's left of Lake Texcoco."

His eyes scanned the height of the cathedral as we stood in front of it. "The Lake . . . that is only the beginning. And you will experience it. Do you know about Huitzilopochtli and his sister Coyolxāuhqui?"

"No, but I do know the goddess, or at least a large stone carving of her, was found here. It's in the museum."

He turned to me and looked me in the eyes. "She tried to have her unborn brother killed because she thought her mother had been having affairs, and in turn he was born in full armor ready for war. For Coyolxāuhqui's betrayal against him and their mother, he chopped her into many pieces and then cast her head into the sky. He is the sun and she the moon. A cycle which he always wins. He refused to be vanquished by *her*."

His lack of expression startled me. The emphasis on 'her' made me feel uncomfortable for reasons I did not really understand. But I was exhausted from experiencing fear day after day and dismissed it.

"That is some story. Why don't we go inside?"

And without hesitation his grim, dark demeanor became light again. "Absolutely!"

The church lay as silent and still as a bedtime prayer. Not a single person sat in the pews. The candles flickered as we entered with the faint scent of incense clinging to the air. Long shadows from the pillars looked like looming ghosts who had given their lives to create this place. I couldn't help but notice the decrease in temperature. The cold was uncomfortable, but I had nothing to cover my exposed arms.

"This way," he said.

Gregory led me to a bolted wooden door at the back of the church. He took a key attached to the side of his University of Pennsylvania backpack. I thought I remembered reading he was from UT Austin. Maybe it was from a friend. We proceeded down a narrow stone spiral staircase that looked ancient with a string of exposed light bulbs overhead. I followed his lead in the cramped space. The air felt warmer, and damp, the further we descended. I could smell moisture and a sour staleness in the air I tried to ignore.

At the bottom there was a tunnel about five feet in height. "Watch yourself," he said before slinging his backpack to the front of his body. I could easily fit, but he crouched through until we entered an open chamber connected to more tunnels. Instinctively my mouth opened in wonderment, and I stepped further into the room. Stones carved with images of the Gods lined one wall. Skulls and bones neatly created adjoining walls. You could see the jagged seams of the craniums, some with large gashes from a head blow. Black pits that once held eyes stared back at me. That is when I heard Gregory whisper.

"A final sacrifice so I will live. So *he will live. He will not be defeated.*"

I turned to see a flint blade with a bone and turquoise handle in his hand. Those beautiful eyes that drew me in were as black and hollow as the skulls watching us. His body blocked the tunnel leading back to the church. I was trapped beneath the city, inside a temple used for this very purpose. I had allowed myself to be led to my own grave.

There was only one way to go—deeper into the temple. I had nothing on me to fight him with, so I bolted down one of the bone-lined tunnels towards a light hanging by a wire. Then I saw clothing crumpled on the ground.

Before me the decapitated and dismembered parts of a woman lay in a circle exactly like the stone carving. It wasn't a precise job with the skin and veins appearing like a dirty torn cloth. The bones had been hacked by the look of the uneven cuts. The dirt surrounding the severed body parts glowed bright crimson but was not wet. My eyes widened at the sight, fully understanding what I was seeing, a physical representation of the great stone disk found here. One of the greatest finds and truly magnificent. Gregory recreated it in flesh. Was Gregory trying to capture the power of this God Huitzilopochtli through sacrifice? And I was Coyolxāuhqui? The defeated woman time and time again. I tried to control my gag reflex and fled because I wanted to survive. The past five years had taught me that.

If I wanted to live these past years in quarantine, then there had to be those stuck behind a screen all those years stewing in their pent-up frustration turning to hate. Probably even meeting others with those same twisted ideologies and desire to destroy.

I glanced back. He followed slowly, still chanting in a hypnotic, possessed state, "A final sacrifice so we might live." It was as if he knew I had nowhere to go. Panic and fear surged, pounding in my head and neck. I called to God. *I don't want to die. Give me the strength to live. Show me what I need to do.* The deepest trench in my heart acknowledged this was most likely a futile ask. Just ask the dead buried here, and those out there over these past five years. No ears listened down here just as I knew no one heard humanity. It still made me feel better to utter the words.

Ahead, I could see the tunnel diverted into a dark space. Perhaps I could hide. Maybe I could wait until morning when work resumed. I ran towards the darkness that was beginning to consume the illumination from the single light that was further and further away. I put my back to one wall, feeling stone and bone beneath my fingertips. I inched deeper down the dark tunnel until my hand hit something hard, wooden. I bent down and grabbed it, bringing it to my chest. The top felt metallic, both ends spiked. Some luck. The only sounds were his footsteps, his voice, and the distant din of cars above my head. Sweat slid down my spine and between my breasts. I couldn't tell if it was the ambient temperature or my fear bringing a sudden fever followed by chills, a thousand breaths of the slain uttering their last words upon my skin.

A light approached along with his steady voice. He had a flashlight attached to his head. I moved deeper until I hit another wall. A dead end. I would have to fight. Blood would be spilled but it wouldn't be mine. In the light I could see I held a pickaxe. It was small, the kind you use on soft dirt or rock. It would have to be enough.

"Come closer and I will use this!" I shouted.

He cocked his head with a wide grin exposing his teeth in a predatory way, and then he rushed towards me, dagger in hand. I raised the pickaxe ready to strike. My entire body tightened. Before he could reach me, I swung with all my strength, screaming out my fear and grief in the process. My heart felt like it had burst at the veins and my scream didn't stop until it pierced his skull, sending his body against the wall. He slumped to the ground. Blood oozed from the wound in a steady stream and brain matter clung to the tip of the axe when I yanked it out. But it did not pool. The earth soaked up the red liquid, drinking it with vigor.

I used my foot to move the dirt around. There were stones beneath. I continued to drag my foot through the dirt, exposing more stone underfoot. At my side a crimson thread of blood ran the length of the seam of exposed rock. I continued to kick up dirt with the trail of blood following me. The path led to my right, further from the entrance. I had to see where this led.

I must have walked for forty-five minutes before I heard the light chime of trickling water. Maybe it was a pipe with the sewage system. The louder the sound of water, the faster I kept sweeping the stone path with my foot.

And there it was. It was the chamber. I knew this because the photos on the internet had the same handwritten sign with technical information on the dig that didn't matter much to me now. The only thing separating me and the vestiges of Lake Texcoco was a flimsy piece of canvas.

I pulled it aside. Candles were nestled in the wet dirt just at the entrance and illuminated the murky swamp gurgling from some unseen hole in the ground. Gregory must have prepped the candles before meeting me. Patches of algae floated on the top. I took a step closer. From the dark water small lights began to brighten with the speed of flickering fireflies.

As I watched I could feel breath against my neck and my skin turn hot. "Mestiza blood, you have arrived. Many thanks for the final sacrifice. My brother has kept me dismembered for far too long and now it is time for my pieces to come together again. For all your pieces to be brought together. I did not seek to kill him at birth because of the shame of our mother conceiving without a husband. I sought to end him because I knew he would keep me subjugated and dismembered for an immeasurable time. It came to me in a dream. Unfortunately, our battle left me in a state of incompleteness. I'm sure you have felt this. You will no longer experience this. The time for us has arrived."

I turned to see a woman, her skin as brown as mine with glowing moons for eyes. She appeared exactly like the relief found in the temple. Naked except for a loincloth, her breasts hung low. There were thick stitches made from sisal where her limbs had been rejoined.

"What are those lights in the water?"

"They are the souls of the gods waiting for life and the souls of the many women dismembered over time."

The moonlight in her eyes pulled me closer like a tide. I had no control over my thoughts as she gifted me with a vision that gave me a sense of power and peace.

In her eyes I saw the end of feeling afraid of my body and any fucking Huitzilopochtli trying to manipulate or mutilate me in any way. All the pieces of ourselves, our flesh, our love, our power, our innocence, would be returned. She would see to it.

"Why don't you go inside and find out what stories they have to tell?" I took a step back. "About what? I'm afraid."

"Don't be afraid of your home, or the secrets of Aztlan."

With one foot in front of the other I made my way into the dark ancient waters. I was ready to see where Lake Texcoco would lead me.

DIVING FOR PEARLS

It was a moment of rest and silence at dawn. There was no one to force me to do anything. I watched the rays of sunlight rise across the calm waters and wished I could float upon the back of that light. The day would be long again. The measly portions of oysters and dried fish hardly kept me satiated, or any of our bellies full. Most of the divers appeared skeletal from lack of enough nourishment compared to the work they were forced to do. I was lucky to have a small amount of cassava bread every morning. This I shared with him on the days he could join me. On days like this I wondered what was beyond the horizon. Where could the ocean take us?

We were pearl divers. Our bodies given to the ocean day after day. Each pearl cost a life, and it took so many to string on the necks of the Spanish men's wives. The largest were sent to their king across another vast ocean. Their Brown mistresses got nothing for conceiving or raising their bastards.

I was the exception. There was no home for me to be domesticated in because my father and brothers fished and dove for pearls. Only my father remained though. My brother dove and never returned. No body washed up on the shore—they rarely did—and the merchants asked no questions except who would replace this lost commodity. The ocean possessed enough of our tears so my father and I said a prayer to the setting sun when we knew for certain he would not return. Then there was me. When my father proved he could not keep up the pace with the younger divers, he was forced back into fishing to feed the soldiers the best catch and left us with whatever remained. I took his place in diving.

There were not many female pearl divers. That is how I met *him*, Itzli. His name suited him because it means obsidian knife. He loved his blades and knew how to use them. He came from a family of once proud warriors until our defeat. Pearl diving was only something he did for a sense of fun and danger before *they* arrived.

His long limbs and strong body could dive deep. He wore his graying black hair in a long braid that fell to the middle of his back. His eyes were blacker than the deepest caves beneath the waves. Looking into them is where I found a piece of my inner broken shell. His eyes, that body, were a landscape of sensual delights. The first time I laid eyes on him I didn't know if I should run and hide from an incoming storm or tell him without knowing him that I was his for as long as we had left in this strange fate we found ourselves in. At the very least we could experience some pleasure before our bodies and souls were captured by the ocean.

Opening shells also kept him out of the water longer than most. Helping my father unload and clean fish helped me escape too much time in the water. Unlike other divers, our skin remained intact without the usual boils and blisters caused from the salt, blows from the merchants, and sun.

No one wanted to stay underwater too long, but soldiers sat in a boat monitoring the divers. Once the divers bounced above the waves they were greeted with a club to go back down. The pressure beneath the water took its toll on everyone. Only the sturdiest survived. We couldn't keep track of who lived and died. But that was not the worst part of it. Our dead were simply weighed down with rocks and thrown back beneath the waves to be consumed by the sea. We swam among the rotting corpses of those we knew and of strangers. Stripped of what made them human made them look the same down there despite each one in a different state of decay. Some with an arm floating free reaching for the sun to scoop them to salvation instead of this water hell that was actually once quite beautiful. Others were half-eaten by large prey. A few became homes for crabs and fish.

What woeful lives we lived. The Spanish didn't understand that we were not disposable. Pearl diving required a certain talent and years of perfecting. Itzli and I learned while we were still young. Pearl diving should only be done when time and weather permits.

On that day of first meeting, water from his long braid dripped down his bronzed chest as he sat on the ground prying open a basket full of oyster shells. He wielded his blade with such precision he could open shells faster than anyone else without injury. His lean muscles twisted with the sensuous movement of a water snake. It was impossible not to imagine how it would feel to be coiled in his embrace or my lips pulling back the skin of his old life so he could welcome the new with me in it. I had to bring this beautiful man my oysters. The craftsmanship of the flint blade in his hand was impeccable. The handle was bone from what could have been an animal or human. Until then we had only been in each other's vicinity in passing. He was leaving, and I was returning. Fate aligned at that moment. I lay my basket with oysters next to him and kneeled on the ground. He stopped opening the oyster in his hand and looked into my eyes. "That's a good haul," he said.

I watched his full lips without knowing what to say next. "I guess . . . I'm Paz."

He nodded. "The fisherman's daughter."

My stomach clenched with the thought that he knew who I was beyond this moment. The hot sun felt as if it had turned up enough degrees to instantly evaporate the water on my body.

"I'm also just me." I pushed my basket closer to him. He touched my hand as he brought it towards him.

There was no looking him in the eyes again, so I shifted to his blade. "I love that. Can I touch it?"

His squinting eyes darted to see if anyone was watching. "Sure." From that moment a new story was in the making for our lives. Don't know how I knew this, but I just did. His lingering touch and gaze felt as good as an ocean breeze at night. I was wide awake in his presence. His stomach grumbled.

"You hungry?"

He chuckled, "You heard that? Yes, I haven't eaten since last night."

I looked around to make sure no one could hear what I was about to say. The merchants, divers, and soldiers all went about their business. Asking him to join me alone was a risk, but I risked my life day after day. This seemed small. If he said no then that would be that. However, I had a sense of a strong tide pulling him closer to me and he would say yes.

"When you are done tonight, meet me by the bay where we store the boats. No one goes there after leaving for the day. I have cassava bread and fish. Let me feed you tonight."

He smiled. "I will be there."

The merchants became loud trying to get the divers taking a rest back into the water. I jumped to my feet and headed for the cliff edge before one of them could put their hands on me.

That evening I stood by the boats and watched the sun setting the ocean on fire in the shape of a fish tail. Part of me wondered if he would show up, or if he was just being polite.

And then I saw him. His hair was dry and fell to his shoulders in soft waves. And those lips, perfect in shape and perfect for exploring every inch of me that ached upon sight of him. He looked like a sun or water god come to grant my wish, made perhaps in a previous life.

"You came."

His bright smile accentuated the creases at the side of his eyes. "I wouldn't pass up a meal with a woman like you. How often does that happen. And another pearl diver at that."

I sat in the sand and took from my leather satchel what food I had to share with him. "I'm sorry it isn't more."

He sat next to me, closer than I expected, but I loved that. "This is a feast. But you know this."

We ate side by side while watching the sun set. In that moment it felt as if life was perfect, and the invaders didn't exist. As it became dark, I could feel a chill with the sea breeze. My body trembled. Instinctually, he wrapped one arm around me and brought me close. "We can't have you shivering."

Our eyes fixed on each other. Without words, his lips were on mine. His kisses quenched a thirst that never could be satiated. In my mind I hoped this was my gift before I left this earth. I slipped my hand between his legs to feel him harden. With my other hand I pushed him to the sand. He acquiesced to my gentle touch. All I wanted was to taste him. His sweat, his semen, his tears, all the salt of the sea he stored in his body I wanted in mine. My lust for him had transformed from an inescapable whirlpool in my mind to leaving me wet and inviting. He slipped inside of me with an ease of lifetimes in the making.

After that night of lovemaking there was no separating us. The couple of pearl divers who should not be but were because of circumstances beyond our control.

We lay beneath the new moon after another day of diving, fish cleaning, and oyster shucking. I untied the leather around his waist where he carried his blades. My mouth searched his hip bones and taut stomach. I loved his tall frame. His limbs tangled mine as did his hair. When it brushed my mouth I could taste the salt of the sea. Effortlessly he surrendered every delicious morsel of himself into my mouth and body. In return my body was for his to tie and untie in knots of ecstasy over and over again. After, we would lay with the night breeze to cool our heated flesh.

"I wish we could escape to the stars. They aren't forced to do things they don't want," I said.

He remained silent, his face looking darker than usual.

"One of them spoke to me," Itzli said.

I raised myself from his chest to look into his eyes. "What do you mean?"

He reached for one of his blades that were never far from his grasp and touched the point to his knuckle to pop a blister. I grabbed a cloth and dabbed the puss and blood away. "You know I'll believe you, my love," I said.

"You really want to know?"

I kissed him. Our kisses were the secret language only we knew.

"All of you in the water now!"

Itzli stood at the edge of the cliff with his hand on the leather belt around his waist that held his flint blade. The only reason he could carry such a weapon was his skill with opening oyster shells. So many slashed through their hands in the process. Some healed and others became infected and died. The ones who forced them to dive injured or not wouldn't dare risk their own skin. It pained him to see the agony on the faces of those who had to swim with open wounds and sores on their body.

He had a family to protect, at least those who were left, and there was Paz. He didn't allow his eyes to stray far from her when the Invader men were around. But under no circumstances was she to be touched according to the merchants. Both of them were given a little leeway because of their skill in diving the deepest to bring in the largest and most unique pearls. Paz was his pearl.

She treated him like he was hers. In a cave not far from there was where they sometimes made love. Their bodies in desperate need of heat from the icy perils of diving. She wrapped her short but muscular legs around his waist with her arms thrown around his neck. The crash of waves on the outer wall of the cave matched the passion they possessed for each other as he thrust inside of her, and she met his insatiable desire to feel himself deeper inside.

A tap on his shoulder brought him back to the cliff. It was time. He pushed to the farthest depths because that is where he could get a good oyster with a fat pearl and keep the merchants off his back. It bought him a little time because although these new masters were hideous and dangerous in their cruelty, they also knew enough not to kill off their best divers.

He broke through the frigid waters. His entire body became encapsulated by this other world with its own rules about life and death. The muscles in his arms worked hard against the current until his hand was pulled back behind him, the feeling so jarring he nearly opened his mouth to scream. He looked in the direction and saw one of the bodies of the dead, discarded divers. An eel crawled out of one eye. Flesh peeled back from the bones like floating seaweed. And then he heard it in his mind.

Itzli, you are a blade. A cleaver of souls. That is your gift. Bring them to us. Split them open like oyster shells. And in return you can have this . . .

An eel brushed against his ankle causing him to look down. His eyes followed it swimming towards the feet of the dead diver. An oyster shell larger than he had ever seen lay at its feet. He grabbed it and swam to the surface before he remained below forever. Eventually it might happen. At the very least, he'd found Paz before the end.

I nuzzled closer into his bare chest. His heart didn't seem to beat faster than normal. He was serious with his tale of hearing our dead speak to him. The entire seabed where we dived was a coral of human bones.

"Killing them will mean certain death."

He turned to me and kissed me on the forehead. "We already are facing that, my love. How much longer do you think we have? We can never have children together, but we can create something memorable in blood. For our people. For the divers at the bottom of the ocean."

I crawled on top of him. His beautiful thick lips curled to a smile as I took the blade into my hand. "You won't do this alone. Let me be on this journey with you. Now that I have found you, there is no turning back."

Both his hands rested on my hips. "I have something for you. For us."

I smiled. "What is it? I already have you. When there is no cassava left, I will eat you."

He reached to his leather satchel and pulled out an oyster shell, but it wasn't just any shell. It was larger than I had ever seen, nearly as large as one of his hands spread to their limit. He had made it into a weapon, a blade. The soft point where the two parts of the shell usually connect was sharp. The point could easily slice through fish, or a man. The iridescence could just be seen when I lifted it towards the moonlight.

"Thank you. Is this for my fish or to carry out the wishes of the dead?"

He took the blade from my hand and placed it on the ground next to us. "It can be for whatever we choose. I need time to think of a plan. If we go on the run, I'm not sure how far we will get."

"I know. I think about how we could escape together . . . Is this the oyster shell the dead diver gave you?"

"Yes, and I buried the pearl, a black pearl, near our cave by the boats. It's in a leather satchel. It is wedged between the rocks when you first enter."

I nodded. "For now, let's get rest before another day under the sun and in the water."

We had more time than most together, working together in the open and making love at every opportunity in secret. My father had his suspicions, but turned a blind eye because he knew Itzli was a good man. We could take care of each other.

The merchant named Alonso stood with one soldier beside him. Both were dripping in sweat and swatting insects from their wet skin.

"I know you probably don't understand the importance of this but there is a very pressing task at hand. We must provide a portion of the dowry for your Sovereign's daughter. We need the brightest and best pearls as quickly as possible. Be prepared to work hard. It is also the king's wish to give the queen a magnificent gift for her birthday, and she requires a very grand gift. It is up to you all to find it."

Itzli and I glanced at each other. This wouldn't end well because I couldn't see how they could demand more from us. How unprepared slaves with little experience in the water would die? I wish I could scream this but knew even if I did it would be lost on them.

"You two." The merchant stared at us. Panic made my nearly empty belly feel sick. Did he know we were involved? Then again at this point I didn't care. It would come out eventually, just like death.

Itzli looked at me again and then the merchant. Something had changed in his eyes. He took my hand in his. I swallowed hard and walked with him, hand in hand. The merchant looked at our display of affection.

"As long as you don't give birth to a bastard, I don't care what you do. You two are my best and that is all I care about. You make sure these others get what we need. I want you both down there. Show them how to dive properly. Don't let them be lazy. If anything goes wrong, it is up to you. Now get us those pearls or I will make sure you can't have each other. You start now."

My empty belly hurt. Being with Itzli came with a high price, the flesh of our brothers and sisters. The coral of bones would surely grow with this added pressure of finding pearls. I was sure this was not what the dead diver at the bottom of the ocean had in mind. Itzli had dived hundreds of other times but never heard that voice again. We never talked about it either.

Two weeks into this new project the voice returned.

The merchants knew the storm was approaching because they refused to get in any of the boats that day. Ours teetered side to side with water rushing in. It was cold when the wind swept past us. The sun refused to shine, perhaps he had seen enough of this torture. Many of the divers coughed and spurted blood when they broke the surface. It was easy in the angry water to inhale it in large gulps. They were also diving deeper for longer.

A young man who barely had hair on his chin floundered in the water. I could see the fatigue in his eyes. I elbowed Itzli who bucketed water out of the boat. "Keep an eye on him. I think we should pull him out. Really, we shouldn't even be out here. I hate this."

The sky was dark gray in the distance but the clouds moved with the speed of soldiers on horseback . . . and would be just as lethal once they reached us. Rumbling filled the atmosphere and the deafening crash of waves surrounded us. In those few seconds of looking away there was screaming from the water. The young man waved his hands before falling below. Itzli wasted no time diving in to help the young man caught in the fury of the tide.

My heart pounded as I searched the water, despite there being zero visibility. I looked up to signal to the other divers just surfacing to get into the boats and go. Lightning lit the darkened sky. "Please bring them back," I screamed to the waves pulling at each other with the viciousness of clawed beasts. Then I looked to the sky that was opening up with rain falling onto my face, "You gave Itzli and I to each other. Give us more time even if it means to serve you."

I took dried fish from the boat and threw it into the water as an offering. It wasn't much, but I hoped it showed my devotion. The pieces were swallowed by the waves upon impact. I grabbed the edge of the boat and waited. Not sure how long I was there because it felt like an entire journey wandering the underworld's gauntlet of tests, but pale appendages soon bobbed above the water. I saw Itzli's face. He shook his head when our eyes met. Then he began swimming hard. A large wave pushed him from behind close enough to the boat for him to pull himself inside with trembling arms. He collapsed shivering from cold exhaustion. With all the strength I had in me I rowed towards the small cove where we kept the boats. But the sea was on our side for the moment. We were pushed to the shore with a violence that gave us speed. I grabbed the bag where I kept oyster shells before climbing out with Itzli. We took shelter in our little cave separated from the world we had no interest in and I made a fire with the remnants we always left behind. With my arms and legs wrapped around him I warmed him in silence as the flames continued to grow. He would speak when he was ready. I watched the storm, and he closed his weary eyes.

As his skin heated to a normal temperature, he sat upright. "That boy didn't make it because he became a sacrifice."

I handed him a large piece of cassava bread from my satchel. "What happened?"

He looked at the bread and tore it in half before giving me back a portion of it. "That dead diver spoke to me again."

Iztli could barely see the boy with the current tugging at both their bodies. Debris covered his field of vision. Corpses danced in the murky, stormy water. He reached out hoping that the hand he perceived was the boy's. The arm tugged back dragging him further and further to the depths. Itzli attempted to break away but without any luck. This couldn't be the boy, not with this strength. Not the way he felt himself cutting through the water with the force of an arrow. In an instant he was thrust up again. He found himself sputtering and gasping for air inside a small underwater cove with just enough room for his head. In the darkness, he could feel the rock scraping his scalp. Never had he experienced the dark until now. It was a space where light was replaced with cold. He couldn't see it, but he could feel wet flesh crawling up his torso until it had him by the throat. Itzli didn't dare move. Sharp nails dug into his skin.

"Remember me," it hissed in his mind. Iztli's eyes stung from the saltwater as he squeezed them open and shut.

"Yes, where is the boy?" he replied.

"He had to come with me. He wouldn't have survived anyway. You didn't bring me any of the masters. I've been waiting." The hand gripped his throat tighter.

"Who are you?" Itzli managed to ask.

"In life I was no one but in death I am all of them."

"What you asked of me is a massacre; not that they don't deserve it, but I want to live my life, too. There are too many of them. How can you rid the sea of every grain of sand?"

"It has been cursed. They have been cursed."

"What? How would you know that?"

The hand loosened. "My mother was a priestess. When I did not return from diving, she cursed this place, a curse that will last until it is cleansed. No one will bear children who will only die. The merchants will all meet their ends. Then she threw herself into the sea to be with me. But there is one remaining task. We could read the thoughts of the divers, including yours. You are on a hunt. My mother says take the black pearl you have buried and give it to the merchants. It will be given to their queen. The curse will pass to her, and she will die. None of her line will bear children. You must do this. But first it must be washed in the blood of one of theirs. After, throw the body to me. The curse will be complete."

"I will gladly take this curse to their queen, but why must we perish in the process? They will seek vengeance. What will happen to the merchants and soldiers?"

"Your destiny will be set once you do or don't do this. You are all just as dead as we are down here. As for the merchants, tell your woman, the one you dive with, to cast her nets while it's still dark and beneath her majesty the moon. Do not eat any of the fish caught. Let the invaders perish from what they consume. The rot of death will invade their bodies."

In the dark there was clarity. Light hit his soul and there was no way forward but to be part of this curse. Just as the diver said before, *he was the blade*. "I will do this."

"Good," it hissed. "Now take a deep breath before the current of our souls takes you back where you belong."

Itzli filled his lungs with the air in the small cave pocket. The hand let go of his throat and moved to his ankle. Without effort his body twisted and turned amongst the strength of the sea. He pushed through until he inhaled oxygen again. Paz frantically looked into the water until their eyes met and melted into each other. Another shove of water beneath his feet took him to where she was.

"Faith is a funny thing. This dead diver wants us to have faith in it and the priests want us to have faith in a God who kills us," I said. "I think I'll take my chances with the dead. I will fish. You spread the word to the other divers not to take their rations. They need to eat something else. One day won't make a difference. Let me tell my father and then I will do it tomorrow night."

Itzli crawled to the two rocks not far from us and retrieved the buried pearl. It was indeed magnificent. I couldn't believe something so light and sensational could contain so much death. I couldn't wait to see this curse, even if it meant I would die.

I returned home to tell my father we would fish at night but couldn't taste any of our catch, and to spread the word no one else should partake in this catch.. Every last one would go to the merchants and soldiers of the village. He gave me a hard stare with his leathered face. The deep creases showed me what he was thinking. Vengeance would be his pleasure.

The following night the moon shined her light upon us. We cast the nets and let them settle, expecting to be there for some time. But this was no ordinary fishing excursion. The nets began to fill quickly. It had to be the dead diver calling on the lethal magic of the hate still lingering in the bones and bodies of the deceased. My father and I had to pull the net up quickly otherwise it would break. The muscles in my arms and legs felt as if they would tear the harder I pulled. For an old man my father did his best, but I worried about him. With one last tug, the net fell into our boat. How beautiful the catch was. The fish with their fattened bodies glistened beneath the moonlight. We could not eat them; however, they looked so succulent the merchants and soldiers would not have any control over their appetites.

"It was a good catch. Now we will watch."

The following morning Itzli helped us bring the fish in large baskets to the merchants and soldiers. Their eyes went wide as they descended on it like hungry jaguars on a wounded animal. If only they had the courage of those beasts. Soldiers, merchants, their leaders from the village all came to take from the large haul. The divers stayed well away. Even if they wanted scraps there was no way to get between the men scrambling to get theirs before it was all gone. Itzli stood behind me with his arms around my waist. He took one of my hands and placed it on the small pouch hanging next to his blade on his leather belt. The pearl.

That night we would slaughter one of them, a little fish to cut and bone for the pearl divers rotting under the sea.

The moon was even brighter than the night before. Soon it would look like a pregnant woman's belly. From a distance we could hear their grunts and wails of torment. The fish were poisoning them slowly. We passed a few dead ones on the path. We held our oyster blades tight as we locked eyes. Both of us knew deep down this revolt may not do much in the long run, but if we were going to die then so would they. And many already were dead. The poison from the sea had wiped out half of the Spanish in the village. The ones left wanted their stolen treasure before they fled. But we knew they had it in their blood stream. It would only be a matter of time before they fell off their horses dead. From the distance we could see a flame from the home of the head merchant, Alberto. The closer we got the louder the retching. I knocked on the door. A village woman opened the door with her nose and mouth covered. In her eyes I could see a knowing. Something not of this world was at play here. "I am here to see Alberto."

She opened the door wider to let me in and led me to his bedroom. There he was, a sodden piece of flesh and soaked clothes stained with vomit and shit. He reared his head towards me. White foam caked the corners of his mouth.

"You . . . You did this! You did some sort of savage devil spell. You will burn for this, witch."

"No! I am here to help. But you must come with me to the beach. There is a remedy. Actually, it keeps us from becoming ill when the catch may be bad. Why do you think none of us are sick? Come with me. You will die otherwise."

The woman who answered the door pulled down the cloth from her face. "She is right. Go with her."

His eyes narrowed as he spat, "Why didn't you tell me this before, you useless woman?"

He stood and hobbled towards me. I had to control my instinct to vomit from the smell of decay steaming from his pores. I gave the woman a nod as I passed her. She had a slight smile on her face knowing he would not return.

Once outside Itzli came into view. "Let me help you to the beach."

The man nodded. "Yes, you are a strong one. I can trust you."

I could see Itzli's jaw clench. He couldn't wait to flay him as I couldn't. Both of our skills, our blades would change things, even if we died after.

Despite the stench of a rotting animal seeping from his sweat, we carried the merchant with his arms slung over both of our shoulders to the cliff. When we let him go, he fell to his knees. Itzli and I wasted no time taking out the oyster shell blade he made for us. Itzli pulled Alberto's neck back by the hair. The man whimpered with no strength left. Seeing Itzli in the light of the moon and a skull in his pupils excited me beyond anything I could have ever imagined. If this wasn't important, I would have made love to this magnificent man right then. He was a true jaguar made flesh, my nightmare and fantasy.

"Are you ready, my love?"

I smiled and brought my blade to the merchant's throat. We sank both our blades deep into his stinking flesh. I kicked the merchant to the ground with my foot as he gurgled blood. Itzli kneeled next to the body and took out the pearl. He held it in his palm before bathing it in the crimson flow. I kneeled next to him so we could do it together. Our hands slid in harmonious motion, like our sex. He leaned over and kissed me hard. His kisses were lethal and sweet. "Put your big pearl away," I teased.

He chuckled. "Now he must be cast into the sea." Itzli stood. He grabbed dead Alberto by one arm to drag him to the cliff side where we dove. The churning waters reached for us as they met the rocks. Together we rolled his body over the edge.

"Have you thought of what's next? How do we get this to their queen? The dead diver left a lot to be figured out."

I looked to the moon and the stars to give me guidance. "Take it to the woman in his home. Let her take it to their head priests. They worship their king and queen like a god. In this horrible tragedy at least some good had come from it. The pious idiot will know what to do. Surely he knows the plans because they all work together in their cruelty."

"My beautiful pearl. That is a perfect plan. Let us go clean ourselves in the cenote and then make love."

Itzli was perfection and knew my heart.

Before dawn we went back to the Alberto's home. Bloated bodies of the Spanish lay strewn across the village. The healthy villagers were already clearing them away. The stink had to go. There had been enough blood, death and shit. The woman answered the door but there was fear in her eyes. Beneath her huipil she handed me a leather pouch. The texture was unmistakable. Pearls. I snatched them and tucked them beneath mine and in the waist of my skirt. "Who is that?"

We wanted the priest, and it could only be him. He stormed to the door. "I came here expecting to find a sick man or a dead man. But this woman says she knows nothing. She let him wander off alone. What is it you want?"

Itzli looked at me. I nodded.

"This was what we were meant to find. For your queen."

Itzli held the cleaned black pearl in his palm. The priest's eyes went wide. More sweat than before was already beaded across his forehead rolled down the sides of his face. It saturated his thick clothing. The heat of the day had begun to bear down on us.

"It is . . . magnificent. Alberto told me about this. I will not delay in getting it on a ship. We will bless it."

The priest cleared his throat and then wiped his forehead with his sleeve. "I will take it now to my fellow priest. A ship is leaving imminently."

"Good. Well, we will go now. There are bodies to bury across the village."

He didn't look up from the pearl as we walked away. For a moment we felt free walking hand in hand. I wanted to spend the rest of the day making love in the shade with no pearls to dive for.

"You have to go. Now!"

Still half asleep I rose from Itzli's embrace. He stirred and sat upright next to me.

"Father, what?"

"The priest is ill and looking for you, all of the priests . . . the ones not dead. They had a huge ceremony before sending the pearl you gave them off with the ship. Soon after they fell under the same sickness as the merchants and soldiers. The priest is telling everyone you did it to him. Both of you will die. Go!"

Itzli and I jumped up. We would try to take a boat to who knows where. We only had time for our blades and a satchel of cassava bread and fish my father prepared. I took the pearls given to me by the village woman who lived with Alberto. I kissed my father goodbye before taking Itzli's hand. It would be light soon and we would have to move fast. To our surprise it was quiet. I hoped it would stay dark just a little longer as we ran past the village and towards our cove.

That is when we heard the gunshots in the distance. We both turned. Three priests were on horseback, albeit not in very good control. They had to be sick. Only the one we met had a gun with terrible aim. He was used to using his words for death and not a weapon. Itzli turned to me. "We run for the cliff. It's the only way. We won't make it to the beach."

I grabbed his arm. "But this isn't the direction of the diving spot. We are too high. We won't survive."

Another shot rang out and we began to run again. My heart pounded trailing behind, but I knew Itzli wouldn't leave me behind.

The sun was rising higher. He stood by the cliff edge with his beloved knife in hand. It was the one his father and his grandfather carried. The breeze caught his hair. The long strands I loved to be tangled in when we made love. I was grateful for the time we had in this life. I loved him. And now on the cliff edge we stood on the precipice of the next life. Soon we would be dead and ready for the next to greet us. I prayed that the Gods would bring our souls together as they had our bodies. If we met each other later in our lives, my heart wanted to recognize him on sight. Would we feel the current upon a single touch or kiss? *Bring us together again, Gods.*

His eyes shifted to gunshots in the distance. It was time. I clutched the bag of pearls. He kissed me once more with his thick lips wet from tears. Side by side we ran towards the edge of the cliff that would lead to sure death. Then we jumped. I allowed my arms to open to release the pearls back into the ocean and the souls caught within their beautiful iridescence. They didn't belong on the pale skin of those women or stuck in some cold gold cross to be worshipped.

I dream I will wake up one day in his arms in another time and in another place where we are free. He will still have his blades and I my pearls or beads. We will still be side by side doing what we love. All of this I saw with the cold surrounding me. I didn't open my eyes because I didn't want to see the dead divers knowing I was becoming one of them. The current tugged at me.

Then by some miracle the sunlight was on my face. I looked around the light waves pushing me towards the line of rocks not seen from above. The bag of pearls floated nearby. A hand grabbed me. It was Itzli clinging to the rocks. I didn't have to dream. We were alive still and this was reality.

"Paz, you won't believe it. I could see one of them look over the edge and shake his head. They think we are dead, and they are the last three alive. There is no way they will live another day. This is our chance. The village will be free."

One of my arms wrapped around his neck as my feet scraped the rocks. I thought of my father. Would I see him again?

"Your deal with the dead paid off, Itzli, and look what I have." I showed him the bag of pearls that bobbed next to me. He kissed me hard again with the gentle waves slapping against our bodies.

"Yes. We live. The queen in their homeland will die soon as will her entire court until it spreads across their land."

"And our village?"

He looked at the rising sun. "I don't know. We can't go back. Let us just live in this second chance. The wind and water will take us where we need to be; just as it brought us together, it will take us places we could never imagine."

I kissed his lips. "Let us find it then. We no longer have to dive for pearls because they are already in our hands. Maybe we will go back to Aztlan."

AT THE BOTTOM OF MY LAKE OF BLOOD

A man named Dante once tried to describe hell. Let me tell you what it is really like.

Hell is an inverted temple, a space to confine their beliefs and fear. Beneath those holy places are the gateways to the many levels of punishment, pain, and redemption. I am beyond redemption. But I don't want or need it. I am what I am.

The last thing you see when you find yourself at the bottom of my frozen lake of blood is the darkness of my throat devouring your consciousness whole. It is not only a punishment for the sinner but also for me. They claw for mercy as they descend into my bowels. My vocal cords and trachea scratched to raw meat. Their splintered bones and nails forever stuck in muscle. The pain keeps me silent. It is because I refused to remain mute, I am cast down. As part of my punishment I've been given three faces when really it is God who is the two-faced one. The absent father.

Gobbling my punishment forever reminds me of my sin. You may think the levels give a hierarchy to sin. I am here to tell you this is not the truth according to God. A beating heart is a sinful heart, and no human can escape their God-given nature or instinct.

The time has come for the truth to be revealed.

Hell is my temple and I wait at the very bottom with my eyes fixed to the ceiling. There is an oculus built by my tormentor. After casting us rebel spirits down, he blew a frigid wind into this cavern before sealing it with a clear membrane. To see and hear the world above. A glimmer of sunlight yet not feeling its warmth. The rays bounce off the membrane and back into the atmosphere. The freshness of rain bouncing against the clear oculus makes me thirst. How I long to wash down the remnants of those I consume. All the moisture down here is trapped in a solid form, including my tears. Torment.

A vast wasteland of red ice surrounds me. It is a lake initially created from the blood flowing from between my legs. The bleeding did not stop until it reached to beneath my breasts. I cannot move from this place. My wings once white now black from frost bite. Teeth chatter curses.

But cracks have been forming. Cycles are a part of life even when the ones who want to keep things the same try to prevent them from ending and beginning again. Permafrost melts from my hot breath. The blood has begun to flow from between my legs. This time it is hot, lava red. Like my soul when it existed. There is a stirring among the nine levels. We can all feel it.

I have spat out the putrid scraps of sinners sent down for me to devour and chew. No longer will I be a thing to be used so God doesn't dirty his precious hands. We have grown weary of being called the tormentors. The insufferable made to carry the weight of suffering. Witches, demons, whores, succubus, temptress, Lilith, savages. I look to the heavens. I shall call upon the God of all that is good and holy to answer for *his* many sins. The world left to slide to disrepute. Let him chew on his own creation. Creatures made in his own image doing unimaginable evil. If they are evil, surely evil must also reside in him.

The cracks are louder, jagged crevices emanating from my body as the ones fallen alongside me have taken up instruments of torture to simultaneously pound against the floor at regular intervals. Their pounding and stomping are accompanied by their cries. The walls shake, disrupting the rings of this inferno. The energy from the fallen one's collective rage cracks the ice. Frost melts at the hot breath from their shouts. Slivers of icicles fall upon my body. Water cascades my face. I open my three mouths so I may drink fresh water instead of the urine and blood of others. I raise my loose hands to the oculus and scream. As I scream, my head trembles, gaining speed. My three faces begin to morph from the violent seizure. My countenances eclipse each other until only two eyes, one nose and one mouth are left. Focus is clear. I am coming into my own. Feeling my body set free, atrophied muscles still have some strength. I extend my black wings, as do the rest of the fallen ones. The prisoners are cut from their bindings and cast into my blood lake to drown.

I climb the rings, my broken fingernails caked with flesh and hair. The cuticles are stained the same crimson as my lips. I am no fallen angel. I am a goddess from a distant universe cast aside. Written out of history and the story. Brown skin, black hair. I climb, we climb. The rumbling of hell, the inverted temple as we reach the top. All at once we will take flight to perforate the reaches of this universe into the next. The light is blinding, the warmth of the sun giving me vigor and speed as I crack through the Earth.

We stand at the top of the temple Uxmal in Yucatán, Mexico. I look down to see the struggling human bodies floating in my blood that rises towards the top. Instead of a stagnant body of water it will soon be a river cascading down the temple steps to water the drying earth. I cannot help but to feel pity before looking away from a place that will never be my home again. From this vantage point, I can see this land. Insects and birds a cacophony in my ears. My faithful legion and I watch in silence. I forgot beauty. I forgot fragility. I can feel hands on my body, reassuring me. Someone wipes away my tears. This world will be mine. It will be restored. God will have to answer for being a non-existent entity, a perpetuator of sorrow who no longer shows himself or his supposed undying love. The world is chaos and he does nothing? The blood from countless wars saturated the roots hanging from between the cracks of our inverted temple. An inferno wallpapered with bloody fauna and earthworms fattened by decomposing innocents. The stones covered in black, red, and orange lichens. The bones of the tortured arranged like the archways and flying buttresses on cathedrals.

The oculus is open, the inverted temple below exposed and the blood lake churning just below my feet. I turn to my legion as the first trickles crawl between my toes. "Go forth and find me sacrifices. Possess the bodies of the wicked, the creators of hatred, the defilers of children, rapists, and murderers, and bring them here. Make them climb these slippery steps with weary legs and sweat-sodden clothing. I shall slice their throats open to release you and their blood before tossing them into the inferno. We will do this until none of the wicked remain and the inferno fills to the top. All of the temples across the Earth will flow with blood. If God cannot purify this Earth, then I will. The old way."

My legion raises their fists and cries out before leaping into the atmosphere. The inferno lake gushes past my ankles. For forty days and forty nights they will take flight. I look to the sky. Sunrise and sunset and God doesn't show his face. Good. He has abandoned this place. It will be mine. In this land of beauty and jungle, cleansed after its brutal history.

The unpossessed have gathered around from near and far but not too close. The humans are calling this "an unprecedented act of God," like I'm some sort of hurricane or tsunami. Then again, I kind of am. It makes me laugh. They want to know who this dark woman is with skin of gold and black wings protruding from her back, daring to be bold on top of a temple. She never sleeps or weeps they say. And I don't.

The possessed file in line like the living dead, unable to break free from their sins and the entities controlling their bodies to the sacrificial stone. Some try to stop the possessed from taking the first step up that temple. They slip and fall before giving up. The possessed are propelled forward by the weight of their deeds. Step by step inching closer to the face of God, me. Goddess of old. I am no idol. Living, breathing black wings create a strong breeze to dissipate the stench of death. I ripped the heads from necks with my bare hands, blood flowing like red ribbons and my fellow fallen ones taking to the sky like an ascending dove to find others. But one bounds up the stairs. She is not possessed, and she carries a blade in her upturned palms. Her eyes are ringed with mascara and lack of sleep. She lifts her hands to me.

"I know you are not God or the Devil. You are something else we can't explain. That is why I offer a gift. I stole it from The Museo Nacional de Antropología in Mexico City. With all the chaos of media gatherings, tourists, and people searching for the missing, it was easy to break in."

"How do you know what I am? And why do you have no fear?"

She held eye contact.

"Because you look how I want to feel when people and things make me feel small. When the little girl inside of me is frightened. You are all I hope to become. I want to be part of something that tears this world in two. Not sure how . . . just a feeling."

In this moment I have so much reverence and respect for this human. Her honesty. I take her gift into one of my large hands as I tower over the humans. It is an obsidian blade with a mosaic handle with multi-colored materials: jade, mother of pearl, conch shell. It is the shape of a warrior dressed as an eagle. "Thank you, my brown daughter. You should go now."

She nods her head and descends the stairs. I lift the blade overhead feeling my determination grow. I look to the trail of humans. Still they come.

Forty days and forty nights.

From my vantage point I keep an eye on the girl. She listens to music while painting the color red on her toenails. She scribbles in a notebook with a look of rapture and determination. She watches every sacrifice, only turning away to sleep or relieve herself. Her friends come to her with food and drink. There is a bond between them. It makes me curious. She wants to be like me, and I like her. I've heard of other gods and goddesses, spirits from the netherworlds inhabiting humans to experience their lives. I decide the young woman from the crowd who brought me my gift will be my new body. We will become one as I live through her in her flesh but still possess all the power of my black wings and gold skin. Obsidian eyes, hair as black as the coat of a Jaguar. At the foot of the temple her friends leave offerings for us fallen ones. In their eyes I can see they are happy to see the wretched tossed into this red pool of justice.

Forty days and forty nights have passed. It is done.

Except for the faithful, the true believers, the crowds have dispersed. A calm has settled over the Earth while new leaders take control and the jigsaw pieces are placed where they belong. The liars who claim righteousness, despots, war criminals, creators of hate, humans who inflict pain on others for their own gratification are all gone. No more tug of war to rip power from their grubby claws. We are at zero. It won't be perfect, but it is better than self-annihilation. Let all the suppressed voices rise.

The time has come for me to claim my new body as a voyager. I will sacrifice myself to live as one of the humans. Let me see if they can course correct. If they do not, then they will have annihilation. I walk down the steps to the young woman I have chosen. She sits in her tent still looking to the sky and scribbling in a journal. It is just before dawn and her friends sleep in their own tents. She sees me approach but is not scared. Instead, she rests on her knees in a kneeling position.

"I want to be a disciple."

I touch her chin. "You are more than a disciple. You will be my everlasting body. I can't walk amongst the humans standing this tall and with these wings. I am not as beautiful as the one they call La Virgen."

"I am no Virgin," she says to me. I like the defiance and spirit inside of her. She is perfect.

I expand my wings. Her eyes are wide, brimming with tears. I wrap my wings around her. As we stand together in the darkness, I place the blade into her hand with my fingers around hers. Without uttering a word, I bring it to my neck and slice clean through. My blood showers her. She parts her lips to receive me. I invade her eyes, ears, mouth and nose. All of my blood enters her body until my skin and wings fall to the ground. Baggage from my past.

I can feel us blinking. Wiping the red away. With new eyes I see. No one has witnessed this occurrence, this day of blessing. When her friends wake, we will offer them the same opportunity to be united with the other fallen ones. Then together we will spread the true story of the goddess in the inferno.

LOBSTER TRAP

The waters surrounding the islands are cold and rocky. Below the surface the darkness overtakes the light. Thick sashes of seaweed dance with the tide and patches of sea grass floating like mermaid's hair cling to the sea floor and feet of the cliffs. Bathers rarely venture far. Even if they did, we would never harm them if they left us alone. A silent respect. The only ones who dare are the fishermen. Greed is bold. Arrogance is fearless. We now know they set their traps in no set pattern to confuse us at the mid-point between the shallows and a deep-sea floor ridge. Many of us were lost until we understood what they were doing. The further out we moved, the further they pursued us, despite the ocean being filled with fish in the thousands. The land blossoming with other means of sustenance.

Their only goal is to trap at least one of my sisters at a time. It is not out of hunger. Oh no, it is sport, ritual. We are as large as the fisherman, sight and mouths evolved more like their species than the smaller version of us. When our life cycle is about to come to an end the eggs stored in our reproductive organs begin to grow. Typically, two survive. The creatures inside spontaneously fertilize. Once large enough, the sac holding them dissolves as they consume it. And then they devour the dying body of their mother who has by then crawled to a safe crevice or cave. It's a peaceful way to go. All the senses are numbed and dim by the time the young nibble their mother out of existence. When there is nothing left, the two lobsters join the others.

We do not know who first declared us a delicacy, a sweet meat to be consumed. Trophy.

It first happened in a tide of confusion, the stormy weather making the waters tumble with natural vitriol. We noticed one of us missing. As we searched, flashing images of the ocean bounced in our collective sight. Outstretched antennae swayed violently as we searched. Then we saw her in a knitted box. She struggled in confusion. Her mighty claws hitting the sides to find a weak point to escape. We could hear her wailing in our single consciousness.

Escape. Let me out. I'm scared.

We rushed through the water as fast as we could before seeing the box rising from the waters with her trapped inside. We couldn't get to her, couldn't help her. We remained helpless as she disappeared into the air, a dark silhouette against the sunlight.

Eventually the waters calmed. Until another one of us disappeared in the same way. None of us ventured far alone after that, afraid of finding one in our path. We learned to live with this fear like the constant sound of the sea trapped inside of a conch shell. It became maddening for all of us. A tight net around our consciousness. Something had to be done. This was not a natural state of existence. We had not evolved any defenses against this predator. Our claws and teeth meant for the creatures down here.

After the last disappearance, I took it upon myself to see what happens after we are taken from our habitat. My sisters waited and watched in our nest in one of the underwater coves carved below the cliffs. I climbed the sloping rocks not far from the long piece of driftwood where they tie their floating vessels. The last of the sunlight in the sky would help me see. But we evolved with heightened senses to survive. I knew I could hide in the shadows. They never ventured out as the sun fell into the horizon. My antennae holding two of my eyes rose from the water, leaving most of my body still covered.

On the driftwood they took turns inspecting and prodding our sister clinging to life outside of water. Bubbles and foam oozed from her mouth. Her long-segmented tail flapped against their legs. She wanted to be cast back to the place she belongs, free. Their smiling sunburned faces laughed with each other. Their skin peeling like scraped fish scales. Unlike us, their bodies are soft. As soft as an urchin without a shell. A cave with driftwood walls as white as a pearl stands in the distance with a spike jutting to the sky.

A large clam shell that is not a clam shell stands where the sand meets soil. Heat, like vents at the ocean floor, burn beneath it. A group of them spill out of the white driftwood cave as it opens. They gather around to watch my writhing sisters be pulled towards the round hot boiling thing. Something like braided seaweed is wrapped around her tail. She is lifted into the air by a large object, made from the same material they use for their boats. Then she is lowered into the boiling clam shell. Screaming. I want to look away, but I cannot. I have to know. I have to see.

Her screaming stops. She is taken out silent and blood red. Red like our eggs. They clap and cheer. The cold water that I usually do not feel invades my body.

She is cracked open from the bottom orifice next to the tail where we store our eggs to the top joint where our body meets our neck. Ten arms hang lifelessly, water and seaweed still clinging to her. They clink shiny objects and sing songs about the treasures of the sea while we weep for the ones we lost. Our screams and wails carried away by the constant murmur of the tides. Waves hitting rock.

I have seen enough and slip beneath the sea. I sink inside as my body moves in weightless sorrow to meet my sisters.

The seasons are changing. They will begin to catch and store as much as they can for when the waters are too dangerous. We have a plan. They are not the only ones with thoughts and souls. When the fog rolls in, we will set our own trap. We curse the traps they set for us so they might stuff their bellies and grease their mouths. Make more of themselves to move across the coastline. We evolved at the depths of the water. The elders say we are drowned humans cast from the pearl-colored driftwood cave. Mermaid magic gave us life again because in life we left them offerings and worshipped them. Was this the reason our ancestors were tossed into the waves that would swallow them whole with no hope of returning? Yet, fate decided they would be reborn to evolve and built to withstand time. Although the mermaids left long ago. My fear is they, too, became caught in traps. Perhaps some are left. I would like to find them one day. But whatever they may have done to us, even the sharks know to steer clear because we hunt in packs. If you see one of us, twenty more are waiting to attack. The fisherman are not the only ones with a cunning nature.

These fishermen are not natural; they don't belong in the habitat below the water, yet they have claimed it and all its contents for their own. Even the largest of us cannot escape. You can smell burning whale blubber for days. No care if a calf is left without a mother.

The deep ridge is further out than they have ever set their traps. Day by day we inch closer to the ridge. They pull up their traps in disappointment. The following day a little further. Once they are beyond the ridge, we wait. As they retrieve their traps, we use our great bulk to pull in the opposite direction, deeper into the water beyond the ridge. Mouth to tail, pulling harder on the trap until their vessels capsize, releasing the blood and guts they use to capture others into the water. As their soft bodies flail in the current, that is when the sharks move in. The waters beyond the ridge are dangerous, no one escapes. No one survives the jaws of mako and great white. The hammerheads gnashing, wild with hunger. We crawl to the ridge and watch them become the delicacy. Their final moments in fear and panic as they are torn in different directions by the predators of the sea. Strings of flesh and sinew pollute the water. Their blood and meat also become our meal. It's satisfying, but soon it makes us all crawl to the dark corners to rest. More come to feast until nothing is left of the fisherman.

When it is dark above the water, a bright light can be seen like the ones sometimes attached to the fish in the deepest parts of the sea. This light becomes thinner and thinner until it is bright again. We stay below ignoring the cycle of the light. None of us can move as our bodies ache. Then something brushes against my antennae. To my surprise, my sight has become clearer. Next to me is a mermaid. Her fingertips run the length of my body. The segments of my tail crack back to life. It causes me to stir. The others are stirring as well, their previous lethargy fading.

It's an instinct-led crawl to the shallows. Our systems are full of the blood and floating flakes of flesh. The water becomes lighter and warmer. My antennae feel strange because my sight is clearer than before. I can sense many others behind me. They, too, are being led. There is splashing all around caused by human feet. I think they are trying to flee as we take up the entire beach. There are other mermaids. My antennae shift to the right. There is a mermaid with a split tail. She almost has a complete human form except the bottom half of her body is covered in thick scales. Her feet are elongated with five mighty curved claws.

We will leave the water together. I flex my claws. And I know there is only one place I want to go: the village.

ASYLUM

The corpses are a bloated, stinking reminder of my station in life. That's how it is in The Asylum, this new demilitarized zone that separates the living from the dead. When you're an asylum seeker you take what you get, and we've got border duty. What was once America is now a wasteland of disease, hunger, feral animals, and things that were once human.

I think I heard the siren. You ready for lunch? C'mon, we can sit in the communal gardens. It smells of oranges and lemons this time of year. I know you're scared, but you don't need to be. You are too young to remember most of it. All of you last surviving refugees who made it here and were allowed in will thrive. No more fighting off the threat of death behind the wall. Even now it remains a surreal dream in my mind. Every day like another page being turned in some cosmic comic book.

You see, a long time ago a wall had been partially built between the two countries. Miles and miles of camps held the line between us and them. Once the amoeba mutated, the cartels threw all their resources into finishing the wall to keep the Americans out. You weren't let in unless you possessed a useful skill, had enough melanin in your skin to take the harsh sun increasing in intensity year after year, or were a citizen from any country south of the border. When the time came for Mexico and the Cartel of Central and South American Countries to decide which asylum seekers they would allow in, all the built-up resentment and frustration between the divided countries foamed like poison from a dying man's mouth.

As you have seen, when the mutants clamor for a way in, they eventually die. Oof, it's fucking gross up close. The smell is worse with that first blast from a flame thrower. Both with the power to knock you off your feet. The stink rises with the smoke, sticks to your hair like cooking fat. Mexico remained unscathed from that damn wall and the heat. We owe our gratitude to the blistering sun.

By the time most of the amoeba-infected bodies made it to the border, they shuffled half-decomposed and slow as hell. The mutants are only as strong as the sloughing muscle left clinging to their bones. An armadillo could outrun them. Those things weren't the threat; it was the tiny creature that could not be seen until it was too late. Entire reservoirs of water left polluted from decomposing flesh seeping into the ground.

To stave off the amoeba infection, the cartel ordered the bodies to be collected and burned before the animals—at least what is left of the stray animals—had a chance to feast on the decaying flesh and make their way into Mexico. There are men whose sole duty is to shoot down buzzards. The crack of high-powered rifles is almost like a call to prayer here. Animal traps lay in wait like IEDs. The rat poison so strong it stings your nostrils when the wind kicks up. That's why we all wear bandanas over our noses and mouths. I already know I'm probably in for an early death. Same for you.

Thank Dios for Felicia García, narco queen turned leader of a Mexico that has never done better for this part of the world. When the Mexican government couldn't pull enough resources together, they reached out to the cartels for help enforcing the closed border. Felicia took this opportunity to strong arm her way into government with the finesse and sense only a woman could bring to a situation teetering towards disaster. Like an amoeba, she took control when the elected officials failed in their political cowardice to make big decisions. Didn't even see her coming as they squabbled over petty shit to stroke their male egos. It was a bloodless coup that happened before anyone could stop it. With a swift declaration of power, she separated Mexico before the infection had a chance to take root like it had in America. Locked and loaded, she ordered a complete lockdown.

I made it just in time. The day I left, I took only what I could carry on my back. I knew my car would eventually have to be sold, or I'd have to sell the remaining gas in my tank. I needed to be light and swift on my feet so I could hide or run at a moment's notice. The cartels took control of the camps at the border because the Americans were losing control everywhere else. Focus shifted to closing the cities. The cartels patrolled the area; those things were on the loose, infected animals ran wild, also biting and infecting. People took whatever had value as rationing became difficult to enforce. Half the rich fucks fled to Europe, but many didn't make it out before the rest of the world closed their borders. Even private planes had to turn back or be shot down before reaching foreign airspace. When I reached Mexico, I gave up my car, what little jewelry I had on me, and showed a guard my family photo album to prove my ancestry, plus a print-out of my DNA that was popular at that time. Second generation on my pop's side and fourth on my mom's side. After all this, I was free to cross into Mexico. They processed me and gave me the job of drone lookout. Mexican American by birth raised in a country that never made me forget I was Mexican first. My skin just a shade too dark to pass for anything but an invader, an inconvenience like a cold sore even though I was born there. Felicia welcomed me like a prodigal daughter.

Maybe I should rewind a bit. I think I'm making it sound too simple. Before you even reached the border a line of military trucks and SUVs with armed soldiers waited for you to pull some shit so they could shoot. If you looked healthy enough to get past the men in tanks, you would be directed to the doctors in hazmat suits. A simple jab to your palm alerted them to foreign bodies in your system. Any traces in your blood, and you were taken to the far side of the desert to be put to sleep on the spot. No questions, no tears. Nada. To be fair, many people accepted this. Nobody wanted to wander around in a stupor covered in black spots with little things swimming beneath their skin, crushing their veins. The mutants embodied the merciless rot the world had become.

The infection begins like a cluster of blackheads on your face. This is amoeba waste. It then painfully pushes through the pores and spreads, like mold. The waste contains spores that cling to their host and travel through coughs, sneezes, bodily fluids, or touch. Eventually the creature takes over the brain and gives only one directive to the body: infect others, spread. Within a few weeks, the body decomposes as the amoeba eats you from the inside out. After a while, you are walking around with half your skin hanging off and insides oozing from your ass. You are a walking amoeba, a mutant.

Mutant bodies and infected animals burn day and night in an area called The Pits. The flames and smoke remind us of the light Felicia has returned to our great nation. Don't look at me like that. The tales are true. Seen it with my own eyes, with goggles of course. Not even the scavengers, human or animal, dare to go to The Pits. You have to piss someone off real bad to be assigned there. A great number of politicians who didn't leave the U.S. in time or make it as far as Canada tried to bribe their way into Mexico. Felicia was having none of it. But like a glamorous telenovela villain, she had a plan. Make no mistake, she is no villain; she is a savior queen. These enemies sauntered in and then were sent to The Pits to work as payback. Those who opposed her, dictators south of Mexico who refused to cooperate because they cared more for their own pockets instead of their people—they were pobrecitos in The Pits. Video from the drone over The Pits illuminated every football stadium for us to watch the worst of the worst get marched to hell. People need entertainment. And the Gods need their sacrifices.

In The Pits there is a pocket of water in an old quarry filled with decaying bodies. The flesh decomposes to create a skin of blood and algae on the surface. Seagulls with yellow and red eyes pull and pick at this. There will be a human eyeball in a beak, maybe a finger. They sit, feast, and lay eggs. Around the water there are nests made from hair, torn clothing, and plastic. Little eggs nestle inside. As long as the gulls remain in their little world they are not shot down. Those sent to The Pits are not executed. No, they must sit by the flesh water until death comes for them. The gulls are aggressive and will pick and peck at them.

Felicia didn't make many announced appearances because she wanted to see how the new nation operated without her watchful eye; however, she always made time to address the people every Friday night. Her speeches were recorded and would be sent all over the world for everyone to see what was occurring here.

She walked up on stage in heels and a bright red suit tailored to her curvy frame. On other nights she wore boots and jeans. Her makeup was impeccable with the blackest eyeliner winged from the corner of each eye, some lip gloss and maybe foundation. It could have just been the sun giving her that glow.

"My people, my friends. From what I hear and see, you are all doing a wonderful job considering the circumstances. You should be cheering for yourselves. All I am doing is ensuring that we all survive and make this a better place. I've read from other parts of the world that I am ruthless or unqualified. This makes me laugh, considering who is writing these things. It is the very people who exploited us and took advantage. They are angry they no longer hold us on a leash. So I say to you: Keep working together. Let's make this the best nation we can together. I am in service to you because you are in service of each other. Everyone will get what they deserve in the end. Just look at The Pits."

It was then the crowd went wild, her wicked smile a dark gaze straight into the camera. Then she went back to work protecting us.

My job today is to stand in a turret along the wall looking at far distances with drones. If we spot packs of the mutants or the barely living, we alert guards on the ground who ensure whoever approaches doesn't get too close. If they appear to be living, we meet them and see if they are of any value. You must have value. There are no family names, bank accounts, companies, business cards. There is nothing but what you can do for the survival of the Cartel of South and Central American States and Mexico. The new super power of the world I am proud to call home.

I remember the first time I genuinely felt sorry for some of them. The Others.

As I passed through the safe zone, a family begged the guards to be let in. Their pale white skin blistered from waiting for days to get this far into processing. The asshole guards toyed with them. The family had two small children who looked malnourished and dehydrated. One of the guards I knew, Francisco, called me over and stuck an elbow in my rib, "What you think, mujer? Should we let them in?"

I couldn't look into their pleading blue eyes. Instead, I stared at the scruffy shoes of the children. "Let them in, cabrón. They have kids. You got kids? Plus, it's almost harvest time. We will need more workers." My job wasn't easy standing in the elements all day, but I did not want to get transferred to harvest. He sucked his teeth and narrowed his eyes as he scanned the family. "What do you have to trade?"

The little girl reached beneath her sock to unlatch a watch wrapped around her scrawny ankle. As she did this the family tightened closer around her. The guard bent down to look into her eyes. This child couldn't have been more than five or six. Her father squeezed her bony shoulder. The guard tried to appear friendly, and he mostly is, but I know what sits behind his resentment. He was only a kid when he was separated from his parents. He sat in a camp for weeks watching other kids from all parts of Central and South America die from a flu outbreak. Yeah, the fucking flu. Tax breaks before outbreaks in those days. Anyway, a riot broke out and he escaped. Been with the cartel ever since. Helped me get fluent in Spanish. So, he was still kinda angry.

"Mija, this is all you have for me? Nothing else?"

She began to cry like children do when they have been scolded even though Francisco spoke in a quiet and calm tone. "Yes. I'm hungry." It was the voice of a little mouse.

"You aren't lying to me? I get very angry when people lie."

Her bottom lip quivered. I could tell she was trying to be a big girl. Save her family. It rested on her ability to convince us they are worthy. "No, sir. Nothing."

The guard inspected the watch then faced the parents. "You're lucky this is a Rolex. Follow the signs for water and processing. The cartel is gonna put you all to work. It's harvest time soon. Our great nation needs feeding. ¡Ándale! Before I change my fuckin' mind."

"Ay, be nice Francisco," I scolded him. "Felicia does not approve of children being treated like that."

He shrugged his shoulders. "You are right. But some things I will never forget, and we shouldn't forget them."

I stood there, watching them all wait in line not knowing how to feel. The family scurried past me in a hurry. The woman turned and mouthed "Thank you" to me. I'm not sure I deserved a thanks because getting into Mexico is just the beginning. You must learn to survive living here. Registration begins your journey. You will be assigned work immediately and found refugee accommodation. Felicia cares for all. I'm a single woman so I need very little. I have a comfortable room with a bed and small kitchenette in an apartment complex. The toilets and showers are communal. It isn't Trump Tower, but I'm alive. No rent due, no grocery bills because we are all fed enough, no cost for my education if I decide to start classes again. Felicia is very clear on her protection of women and children. For her, it's personal. The consequences of abuse are fatal. The Pits, in fact.

How did it all start? Might want to take that last bite of flauta. It's going to sound like a cliché, but it all started with the poorest of the poor. Ain't it always the way. You wanna know how to take the temperature of a nation? Check on the ones left at the bottom. They will let you know if you have motherfucking fever or not. That's why no one bothered to notice or act until it was too late. That would never have happened with Felicia. U.S.

government-sponsored food was cheap, processed crap that looked barely edible, but governments around the world took the hard line that beggars couldn't be choosers. Same went for healthcare and education available to a majority of the populations. All these kids around the globe fell ill. Most of them died. Protests and outrage dominated the news coverage, and committees looked for the source of the problem. Suits with red ties blamed it on the same reasons there were all those E. coli outbreaks with lettuce and spinach in years past. The world called it a bunch of poor people getting sick and spreading their sickness to others.

All it took was one elite boarding school and a shipment of organic milk and vegan sausages to change the tune of those in charge. Seventy-five kids, all sick, and taken to the best hospitals. Whatever was in that milk mutated since it killed those on government cheese.

We now know the free-range, super-cared-for, special cows giving the one percent milk were drinking infected water from a pond located on their idyllic home. The same company also ran a beef processing plant with less-than-hygienic practices that hired illegals at an alarming rate. Turns out whatever used to process the beef and their vegan sausages was not fit for human handling. They were bringing in illegal immigrants because the desperate are considered expendable, and the company covered it up. Just like a damn conspiracy film. What did they play last month in the stadium? Some old-time one. Erin Brockovich. Yeah, it was some Erin Brockovich shit going down. I shit you not.

Mija, sometimes when your skin is closer to the color of shadow, that is exactly how you are treated.

For days I lay in bed sweating, scared as hell to eat or drink anything. The situation worsened by the day and my anxiety threatened to take control over my every thought and movement. I didn't want to shower for fear there was something in the water and it would inadvertently splash into my mouth. That is when I decided to get out. Parents passed and no siblings made the choice easy for me. Life inside my home and mind was unbearable. I packed quickly and set off for Mexico because none of this was happening south of the border or in remote places that didn't take part in the food scheme. I'd rather die on a beach in Mexico in a tequila and lime stupor, getting laid every night, or in Guadalajara at the feet of María Natividad Venegas de la Torre, a saint my Catholic father said is related to us. Anything besides a crowd of amoeba-carrying people fighting over a pack of toilet paper. Don't they know that by the time you shit your liver you lose the ability to know how to use it?

After Mexico sealed off its borders, so did everyone else. The Americans left on their own with no allies. If not for Mexico or Canada, all would be lost on this continent. Without the cartels lead by our narco queen, chaos would rule. She has brought the underworld up to our world, which has made the difference to millions of people. The developing worlds have been given the space to truly develop. All of Felicia's guns, goons, and money created a well-oiled machine made for a part of the world on the brink of collapse.

Mexico and South America on the whole have never been more at peace or successful. Bounty abounds. Fun fact: Central America is home to one of the largest pharmaceutical companies in the world. Production rivals India. They have plants all over. No, not recreational drugs, but shit for the shits, headaches, and antibiotics, to name a few. All in our brown hands, including the priceless drug to kill those silent amoeba motherfuckers in fresh water. Believe that. A teacher from Guatemala sick of seeing her children suffer from waterborne diseases created a test and a cure. Felicia wasted no time bringing this woman to the border and giving her a blank check to recreate her discovery. All the foreign-owned maquiladoras seized and repurposed to bring hope to the world.

Felicia Garcia brokered deals with the rest of the world to maintain the balance between life and death. Sure, it is a ruthless rule of law that will pluck your heart out with bare fingers, but the rules are very clear. You work, you pay your dues, you don't fuck with anyone's shit, you're all good. Stealing, rape, murder (unless sanctioned by a Jefa) is strictly forbidden. When the shortages hit, the cartels set up a food-for-weapons trade. A dead man doesn't need a weapon and a weapon can't grow maize. Hunger won in the end. Felicia has created a space where only she has the firepower. But there is a freedom in this. I feel safe. It's far from perfect, but it's all we have, a dystopian tale of rotting flesh, heat and salvation in an unlikely place. The cartel goes for the better-feared-than-loved philosophy. Snitches don't get stitches, they are rewarded, so keep your eyes open and your hands to yourself. We love Felicia because she has reinvested everything back into the country. Look to the sky, that building over there. A banner with her dark brown eyes looking down upon her flock like the blessed La Virgen. But with gold earrings and red lipstick, hair long and blowing in the wind. One hand carries a torch. Its flames burn bright with small amoebas dying as they touch the flames. In the other a banner with the image of La Virgen de Guadalupe. Thick vertical scars on her exposed wrists show us that she too is a survivor who has bled. She knows sorrow; you can see it in her eyes. She is one of us. If only Diego Rivera was alive to paint a great mural in her honor. She is the Miguel Hidalgo of our time.

North. What about up north? Canada shut their border but had a harder time fighting the mutants without a wall. The cold months kept them somewhat safe as the mutants couldn't withstand the volatile storms of winter. Hell returned with spring. The warmer weather brought animals out to feast on the decomposing bodies until they fell. When the liquid rot seeped into the ground or washed away with the melting snow, who knew where the amoeba would find sanctuary. What is laughable is some of the American politicians actually thought the Canadians would allow them to run the States from within their country, not that there was anything to run. America itself was a living dead thing.

I don't know how many are left in what used to be the United States. The flow of healthy humans has slowed in recent months—lucky for you. I've heard rumors there are some that live in remote areas like the mountains surviving off the land and what healthy animals are left. We had a few enter stating the Native American reservations are bolt-holes that remain safe. Everyone is turned away except for their own. Good for them. Maybe the land will heal itself, and they can reclaim it. I'm not too smart, no fancy degree—yet—but I think it belongs to them anyway.

The amoeba spread exponentially until nothing remained. We watched from the outside thanking the Gods and Felicia for taking us into their bosom for protection. As the States burned, Felicia built a kingdom. That is why we owe Felicia our loyalty. Respect her claws as sharp as the Eagle perched on a nopal cactus. While we work, we recite her mantra: *Love the Cartel and the Cartel will love you back. ¡Viva La Raza!*

Let's get back to work. We have a world to fix.

DAWN OF THE BOX JELLY

Brittany raised her arms above her head as she stared at the crescent moon. A giggle escaped her lips. "Ooh, Neil!" Fingers tugged at her bikini bottom. "I like that. Don't stop."

Neil propped himself next to her bare stomach, admiring the sheen of sweat against her skin that still smelled like tanning oil. He wanted to run his tongue across her body to taste the salt left from their swim in the sea. "Let me tease you. We have all night. Why don't you have another drink?"

Brittany let out another giggle as Neil continued to fondle the tie at the side of her hip with his mouth. "I'm all out." She lifted the upper half of her body and waved an empty beer can before tossing it into the water. Her lips pouted playfully at him.

"I guess we need something else to make you lightheaded. Lay down." He knew this was the moment he had been waiting for all weekend, since their first meeting at the singles mixer.

As he tugged at her bikini bottom, she laid back on the damp towel. A wisp of a cloud was floating over the moon, yet she felt no breeze tonight. The air was still and heavy with salt; all she needed was a shot of tequila and lime to go with it. Slow and sensual R&B played on his phone next to him. The night was perfect so far.

"Are you ready for me to taste your box?" Neil shifted his body to between her thighs.

Yes, she wanted that. It was about fucking time as well. She didn't want to appear fast, but they do say to get over someone you need to get under someone else. The air felt fresh between her legs, like the start she was going to have when she got back home. Vacation romance is always the best because you get the best parts of the relationship without the hassle and compromise that comes after. She closed her eyes, expecting to feel Neil's tongue crawling between her lips. The thought made her clench her anus in anticipation. He better make a journey there, too.

A garbled sound of choking disturbed her fantasy. She opened her eyes half dejected. "Neil?"

He was gone. There was nothing. She grabbed her phone next to her to shine a light around the dark water and jetty. Maybe he slipped to the side to scare her. "This isn't funny, Neil. We aren't in one of your stupid horror films."

She continued to listen for the faintest of sounds. There was light splashing and a dingy hitting the jetty. There was a bump to her left. She swung the light around. Nothing. There was a larger splash in front of the jetty. She slowly moved her phone towards the direction of the noise. The light broke through the darkness to her right followed by directly in front of her. That is when she let out a scream. Neil's body was entangled in what looked like a dozen writhing glass noodles. One was stabbing his mouth violently as the rest of his limbs spasmed in the grip of tentacles. His bare skin sizzled when it came in contact with the creature. Flesh fell off to expose muscle and bone. Every inch of him melted into the creature. He was suspended with arms and legs splayed. Joints loosened until he became mere segmented parts.

Two eyes on the side of a gelatinous square head rolled to her direction, looking straight into the light. Brittany let out a scream hoping someone would hear, but they'd chosen this spot because it was far away from the revelry of the beach carnival going on in the distance. There was no one to hear her cries for help. She dropped the phone to jump up and run when a searing pain snapped at her ankle causing her to fall to her side. Her skin burned with the heat of hundreds of tiny hot pokers plunging into her flesh. It was pulling her towards the edge of the jetty. She managed to swing onto her stomach to claw her way up. But the burning of her ankle took her strength away as she could feel the skin sloughing off. It felt like poison was racing through her veins Another tentacle wrapped around her thigh, further securing its grip. Her flesh melted upon impact. Tears streamed from her eyes as she still weakly attempted to break free. A tentacle raised above her head and daggered into her mouth.

The box jelly now had two bodies in its grasp. Slowly it would digest one of them. Beneath the jetty three smaller jellyfish waited for their meal.

The call was about dolphins floating to shore seared and sliced through with something that didn't appear man-made. There were high dosages of venom detected. The wounds appeared like they were caused by acid. Some speculated a man o' war; however, their tentacles didn't have the capacity to act like a lightsaber.

Guadalupe hadn't planned on going anywhere, but it was a good excuse to get away and they offered to pay for her flight and accommodation. She didn't want to be in the apartment anymore with Rick. He had been away on a golf excursion with his friends for the last few days. Who knows, maybe she would get lucky and receive a break-up email or text while she was away. Otherwise, she would have to end things when he returned. She was finished with placeholder relationships. If it wasn't the one who understood her passion and could perhaps be part of it, she didn't want it at all. The more she became involved in various projects, the greater the divide between her and Rick. And he made it obvious with his backhanded comments that he resented how much she enjoyed research and writing on the subject of venomous creatures. He couldn't stay. No more settling.

The news flashed on the screen. She unmuted the TV.

"*Temperatures are soaring around the globe. Scientists are worried, religious folks are saying it's the beginning of the second coming, and conservatives are telling people to be sure to wear sunblock. Their thoughts and prayers are with those affected by the heat. This is Trevor Miles reporting from—*"

Guadalupe turned off the TV and tossed the remote control to the far end of the sofa. Every night she promised herself not to watch the news because it was more depressing by the day. And now this strange request. The sea temperatures were breaking all known records this year, so much so that certain species of fish were washing onto the shores dead. Restaurants had to import seafood instead of using the local catch. People were worried about the cost of food rising as less became available or there were delays in transport. As heartbreaking as this project was, it was also exciting. They could have hard evidence to further push governments and companies to do more in their efforts to really research what was happening with the climate. Perhaps increased grants for other studies. This was probably the most important vacation that wasn't totally a vacation that she would take in her life. It might even determine if she would decide to have children in the future. As a scientist, she felt only despair; as a human she still felt a small glimmer of hope. She closed her eyes to get a solid night's sleep before her flight in the morning.

The flight from Texas to Portugal was long, and the jet lag would be killer for a few days. When she arrived at the hotel, all Guadalupe wanted to do was check in and take a long nap stretched out in her bed. The line at reception was ten people long and moving at a turtle's pace. She looked out the wall of glass at the back of the hotel. There were men with hairy potbellies and small trunks sunning themselves. Women with tattoos and bikinis drinking large sweaty bottles of water. Kids squealing and smothered in pasty sunblock as they played in the sand. It was beautiful. There were five shirtless men setting up some sort of stage with light. Pop up bars were also being assembled.

April in Portugal is usually dead with unpredictable weather and cold waters; however, with the heat, the Easter crowd was out in full force. British and European teens and families wandered happily around the resort.

A bachelor and bachelorette party were behind her in line. Most of them were already tipsy from drinking during the flight and had drinks in hand as they waited.

After check-in, she finally got to her room. Not even five minutes later she could hear a group of men on one side of her room and a group of women on the other. It had to be the people behind her in line. Thank God for earplugs. Tomorrow she would meet with Liz Porter, the woman from the university who had contacted her about helping with the dead marine animals.

She closed her eyes for a moment before the phone in her room rang. Her eyes snapped open. She rolled to her side to grab the room phone and answered groggily, "Hello."

"Ms. Hernandez. You have a visitor at reception. She says it's important . . . Her name is Liz Porter. Please meet her by the seating area near the entrance."

Guadalupe jerked upright. Waves of exhaustion turned to panic. She slipped on her flip flops and grabbed her bag.

Before she walked out of her room, she passed a mirror on the wall and smoothed out her unwashed hair. Sleep would have to wait.

In the lobby, there were a lot of people milling around, but one stood out because she wore a fitted T-shirt with the logo of Lisbon University. It had to be Liz.

"Hello, I'm Guadalupe."

The woman whipped her head towards Guadalupe and extended her hand, "Liz. We've only exchanged emails. Sorry about the intrusion, but we've had another dolphin wash up. It caused a fuss on the beach. But that is the least of our worries."

"What else has happened?" Guadalupe asked.

"A guy swimming off a boat was attacked," Liz said. "One of his legs was severed. He didn't survive the venom and blood loss. Then a jet skier was pulled off the back of a jet ski. A witness said they saw a large arm, a tentacle, reach out and take hold of the body before they disappeared. No one could back it up and with this heat mixed with alcohol . . . You never know. The authorities are saying he fell off. I assume the body might wash up at some point. We can know for certain then. We also have two missing on holiday. Their friends insist something bad has happened, but the police won't investigate for another two days. Something about young kids holing up for a few days of boozing and sex."

"All right, do you have photos of this dolphin, or can we go see it? Have samples been taken?"

"It's being done right now. I don't know what this is, but it has to be some freak predator. Let's go. My car is still with the valet out front."

The valet had a key in hand when they exited the lobby. Liz gave him a wink as she grabbed the key from him. A small bright blue BMW convertible with the top down was parked in the drop-off section.

"We should only be about twenty minutes in the car. We can catch a cab back later. Big beach party tonight. Can't miss it."

Guadalupe gave her a puzzled side glance. "Shouldn't we be patrolling, or I don't know . . . trying to solve this?"

"You mean waiting? Some of my best ideas come after a couple of shots. If there is something hunting, it should be pretty satisfied for the night. And don't wait for fun to find you. Have it and see what shows up. The city is pretty good about patrolling the waters because of all the water sports, AKA money. Don't worry, this ain't Jaws. It's serious, but we are doing all we can do as part of the university. Carla might be there, too. She's helping with the equipment we need in the water and contracting boats."

Liz flashed her a grin before pressing the accelerator and whizzing off.

The lab was a part of Lisbon University but had a facility on the Algarve for research. Liz led the way inside the frigid, air-conditioned building while Guadalupe continued on to the main lab. It was small but well-equipped. Though the deaths were an awful tragedy, the excitement of solving the mystery engaged her. She forgot her jet lag as she turned around to quiz Liz about the evidence, but Liz lingered in the doorway flirting with a young woman who must have been Carla. Guadalupe waited by the lab equipment, trying not to eavesdrop. Liz was supposed to be bringing back results on the dead swimmer and dolphins as well as the invertebrate specimens that were arriving from different parts of the world. Guadalupe was particularly interested in what was coming out of Australia and the Philippines where jellyfish were known to kill and were common. She cleared her throat to get Liz's attention. It worked. Liz gave Carla a wink before rushing to Guadalupe's side.

"Sorry, I get distracted by beautiful women. Anyway, four of us are going out for drinks later. If you don't have anything cute to wear, come by my room. Lots of attractive people will be there tonight."

Liz had a mischievous sparkle in her eye as she said these words. Liz came from a family of Black scientists all changing the world one textbook at a time.

"I will only go for drinks if we can get through all of the samples. What do we have here?"

Liz turned on her laptop next to the microscope. Carla retuned to the lab with a lab cooler. "Here is what we have from the morgue and the vet."

Guadalupe gave pretty brunette Carla a smile. There was a large scribble of red welts across her belly Guadalupe couldn't help but notice. It looked like it was from a jellyfish.

"Oh, this. This is how I got a job here. Liz helped me when I was stung last year. I've never seen anyone carry so much first aid equipment in their car."

It appeared newer than that, but Guadalupe didn't see any reason why she would lie. "Wow. I'm glad you are all right. How long ago was this?"

"Just over a year. It could have been worse. My heart has never beat so fast. It was really scary to think death was so close. Liz had to use her credit card and tweezers to get the needles out. It's insane to think something so small could cause all that pain. Anyway, hope you guys catch the critter causing this."

Guadalupe opened the cooler thinking . . . *over a year ago*. One by one she removed samples from a local vet that were already prepared for a microscope as were tissue samples from the dead swimmer from the coroner.

"I think we are ready," Guadalupe said.

"Let's take a look, but first check out what's in my inbox," Liz said. "Pictures from off the coast of northern Australia. We all know the man o' war is not a jellyfish. In fact, it is a few different species working together. Well, the man o' wars having been gathering, and there is one massive clump of them here—their tentacles are the size of a small submarine just floating! They have created a new creature of sorts . . . Look how some of the tentacles are intertwined, almost fused in parts. Water samples taken near it were high in runoff from Fukushima."

"Any reported incidences?" Guadalupe asked.

"None. That's what's strange. It just takes what it needs as it floats, but that thing in aggregate has the potential to be extremely dangerous. No one wants to kill it, but everyone is also scared to get very close to it for long enough to study it."

"Yeah, imagine if a swarm of box jelly did that," said Guadalupe nonchalantly. As soon as the words were out of her mouth, she paused. Liz and Guadalupe locked eyes. Guadalupe went for the samples to view under the telescope.

Liz scrolled through her email to find the reports to accompany the samples. Her eyes darted across the text.

Guadalupe went from one slide to another and then back again in quick succession. "Look. The dolphin and the human victim have the same needles."

"According to this," Liz said, "it looks like the same venom as well in both systems. This motherfucker is hungry."

"What do we do now?" Guadalupe asked.

"Well, I tell you one thing. We aren't going Moby Dick here. I'll call the police to see if any other reports have come in or if there's new information on the open incidences. Then we head back to the hotel for drinks."

Guadalupe knew there was not much else right now. The sea was a vast place that kept her secrets close until she was ready to reveal them. She could feel herself coming down from the adrenaline rush. When was the last time she had eaten something? Time to head back to the hotel for a happy hour and bed.

Languid house music played on speakers surrounding a wooden dance floor on the beach. Partygoers danced, drinks in hand. It was good to unwind even if it took a venom of another kind. It felt like the beginning of a dreamy night with the orange and pink streaks of light igniting the sky. Unfortunately, beyond the music and sand some nightmare bloomed beneath the sea. The first glass of sangria went down easy. Everything was cheaper than seafood so they shared a platter of assorted hams, cheeses, and bread. Carla would be joining later.

Liz heaped ham onto her plate and then topped up Guadalupe's empty glass. "So, how did you get into this field? It's quite specialized."

Guadalupe didn't often talk about her family or their beliefs which she didn't share; however, feeling tipsy, she would tell Liz, who seemed more friend than lab partner or sea predator sleuth.

"Snakes. My parents handled snakes in their church service, and I was mesmerized. All my life I had been afraid of things that stung, that could hurt. At church, they proved their devotion to God with poison. Just as the preacher raised a snake towards the ceiling, he was bit. I watched him fall to his knees scratching at his chest before dying in the middle of the service. Everyone screamed. One of the deacons stomped on the snake until it died. Guts and blood squirted in every direction. Watching the poor thing die made me feel angry and disgusted. It just followed its instinct when these people decided to play with it. But then I wanted to know more. How did this venom work? Where did it come from? Did it hurt? How did the snake know exactly how much to inject to free itself from the clutches of a larger predator? All these questions kept me awake. Off the highway between Austin and San Miguel there is a snake farm. I begged to go there and just watch. Biology was by far my best subject because I loved it. In class when the girls would squeal at cadavers, I was ready to see inside. It wasn't easy, but my parents made it work for college. I received a scholarship for grad school."

Liz's eyes sparkled beneath the fairy lights strung around the pop-up bar. "Wow, that is some story. I just like dangerous critters. Don't know why."

Guadalupe took a deep gulp of sangria. "About today. That has to be a box jellyfish, one of the most venomous creatures on the planet, and somehow it has become more aggressive . . . and maybe larger? I wouldn't be surprised if last year Carla encountered a smaller one. We need to catch a few. I need to know what is happening inside of them. The amount of venom found inside the human victim was greater than anything I have ever seen. Can we get someone to fly us down the coast and to the open water?"

Liz stared at her glass and then took out her phone.

Guadalupe poured herself another glass of sangria before taking out a red-wine-soaked orange wedge to eat. "We need to find where they are congregating. They will be budding constantly and who knows how long they live if they have changed in some way."

"I know someone, Dillon, who owns a helicopter tour company. Why don't we go out and see for ourselves?"

"That's a great idea. The sooner the better. If we see anything out of the ordinary we can take a boat out."

Liz raised her glass to Guadalupe. "Cheers. To chasing venom."

Their bodies pulsated through the water, their tentacles floating behind like lace curtains. They would hide in the islands of garbage where they would not be seen. The smaller ones gobbled up the chemicals from the plastics in the garbage. The garbage was like an oasis of armor and shelter. There they could regroup, procreate, feast, and with the water feeling so warm, there were plenty of soft bodies to consume. There was no need to go for the smaller fish that did their best to hide or simply died from the temperatures.

Guadalupe woke up with a dry mouth and spike in the top of her head. When people asked her name had she really said, "Guadalupe, like the river in Texas. You can go tubing on it"?

But she'd had fun. She let go even if it was artificially induced. By midnight, she was dancing to house 80s dance music with a sloshing glass of sangria in hand. Today, they were going on a helicopter. She hoped it wouldn't be too bumpy of a ride with how she was feeling.

There was a knock on the door. She stiffened. Had she told some stranger her room number?

"Guadalupe, it's Liz. I brought coffee. Figured you might need it."

Guadalupe flipped the comforter off her to see her sleep shirt and shorts were on backwards and inside out. Definitely a good night. She opened the door not caring what she looked like.

Liz appeared immaculate without a hint of a hangover.

"How are you so awake?"

"Ha! Maybe I didn't go to sleep yet."

Guadalupe raised one eyebrow while taking a coffee from Liz's hand.

"Not really. I don't kiss and tell . . . most of the time. Anyway, you ready to go on the on the helicopter?"

"Let me just jump in the shower to wake up."

The fresh air and sun felt good on Guadalupe's face. The morning hangover mixed with jet lag was fading. Liz held the camera while Guadalupe looked at the water with binoculars. So far everything appeared normal. The ocean moved with a calm grace. She loved the sea and its complexity. If her soul had a sound, it would be crashing waves.

"Wait, can you turn around?" Guadalupe said into the headpiece.

She nudged Liz. "There . . . it looks like . . . it's a barge of garbage. And there is a smaller pile next to it. We need a closer look."

"On it." Liz adjusted the lens and clicked in quick succession.

"Dillon, is there a beach near here?" Guadalupe asked. "A cove or place the sea drains into the land?"

Dillon slightly turned the helicopter. "Yes, I'll take you to the shoreline. Not many water sports there and it leads into an estuary."

They flew closer to land. "Liz, take photos of everything," Guadalupe said. "Doesn't matter if you don't see anything. We can have a closer look later. And maybe message Carla for a boat."

"Already planned that. She is waiting for us. We can get these photos on the computer before heading out."

"All right," Guadalupe said. "Let's go hunt some invertebrates."

Back in the lab, Guadalupe couldn't stop pacing. "You think we will find anything?"

"I hope so. I have a feeling it's only a matter of time before it strikes again or one of the missing bodies washes up. Remember how they closed all those beaches in Egypt after the series of shark attacks? Really messed up the diving industry there."

Guadalupe usually prided herself on patience because finding grant funding for research was mostly a game of waiting. Neither traffic nor waiting for coffee ruffled her in the slightest, but this was excruciating. The photos of the floating islands of garbage popped onto the screen first. Liz zoomed in to get a better look.

"That's so gross," Liz said. "I knew it was bad, but I don't often have to look at it this close up. What are we searching for?"

"Maybe box jellyfish," Guadalupe said, following her hunch. "They can move with intention unlike the others."

"There!" shouted Liz.

Guadalupe enhanced the image. "It looks like the hood of one, but I think it's a floating plastic bag."

Liz clicked to the next photo of the second heap of waste. Scummy bubbles surrounded the patch of fabric, torn tires, plastics of all colors and sizes. Guadalupe brought her face close to the screen.

"You know I can zoom more," said Liz.

"Oh, yeah, sorry." Guadalupe moved back as Liz enhanced the image. "There. Look. I knew they needed some place to hide and procreate."

A large tentacle, almost lost in the muck, was slung across sneakers that had been viciously sliced open. Smaller heads hid in the scum bubbles almost innocently, but looks are deceiving. They could kill a child. Guadalupe didn't want it to come to that here, but she suspected it happened more times than people liked to talk about. Jellyfish were not as dramatic as sharks, but people, like the ones in her church, didn't respect the creatures.

In the middle of the dump was a bloated decaying foot. A bloody bikini top next to a crown of matted blond hair.

"Holy shit," Guadalupe said, gasping. "I think we have found the missing tourists."

"Fuck." Liz grabbed her phone and called the police.

The sneaky fuckers were eating and breeding in the same spot. Hiding in plain sight. Guadalupe clicked on the rest of the photos, inspecting every inch. Liz hung up the phone.

"We have to go now" she said. "There was an initial distress signal sent from a boat, but it stopped. Carla has been on standby at the dock since we got here. The patrol will meet us at the origin of the distress signal."

Guadalupe didn't really want to see the creature, but something inside of her wanted to pluck it out of the sea, open it up, and show the world.

The little BMW weaved in and out of traffic. Liz knew the streets well. Her music blasted louder than the wind whipping their hair. Horns honked at them as they passed. She had a university parking sticker which allowed her to park anywhere for free. They jumped out of the car to meet Carla on a RIB. The boat was ready to speed off.

"Here are the coordinates, Carla. Go as fast as you can."

"I'm a fast girl who likes other fast girls." Carla and Liz exchanged flirty smiles.

They sped through the rough water which jostled their bodies. Guadalupe held on tightly to the seat at the back of the RIB, worried she would go overboard with each crest they bombarded head on. Her hair whipped across her face blocking her sight.

As they slowed down, she pulled her hair back and saw it. From a distance the catamaran appeared normal, but as they approached it was clear they were entering a bloodbath. A headless body bled out on the deck. The entire corpse was covered in the red, raw, tell-tale signs of a jellyfish encounter. Except these wounds still sizzled. The hand clutched a flare gun that appeared to have been fired. The three other people mentioned during the distress call were not there. Flip flops, beer cans, and phones lay on the deck with blood spatter, but the bodies were missing. Something—judging by the pattern of blood—had dragged them away.

On the corner of the boat a small box jellyfish clutched the edge.

Guadalupe stood at the edge of the boat and grabbed a wetsuit. "Can you get us closer and cut the engine? I'm going to grab it by the hood and then cut the tentacles off as quickly as possible. Hand me the equipment, please."

"So easy," chortled Liz as she tried not to look at the body, but a minute later she said, "Where the fuck is the patrol! I don't feel safe." She looked out to the lonely horizon and shore while Guadalupe unpacked the specimen jars and scissors. She slipped on the thick rubber gloves to handle the small box jelly. The wetsuit would give the rest of her protection.

Guadalupe didn't see anything unusual about this one, but she would know when she took samples from its digestive system and venom.

Guadalupe had just finished securing the cap on the cut tentacles and placing the rest in another container when Carla screamed out.

"Um . . . Guadalupe," Liz said. "Can you hurry up? I think you should look over here."

Liz had her camera out and was snapping away.

There it was. Floating from the front end of the catamaran. The hood of an enormous box jelly, inside of which a suspended body stared back at them, unseeing. The hood broke down each part slowly; pulpy pink good swirled through its exposed system. Nearby, two more massive box jellies broke down the bodies of the other missing boaters.

Guadalupe ripped off the gloves and took out her phone to video it. She recognized the faces from when she arrived. The bachelor and bachelorette party. The box jellies seemed not to notice them, probably distracted by the meals in their bellies. A roar from the RIB made each of them turn their heads as the waves from the incoming boat rocked their own.

One of the box jellies began to approach them. "Fuck. Go now, Carla. Go!" Guadalupe shouted.

A large tentacle reached out and slapped the edge of the boat before Liz revved the engine again. Water splashed Guadalupe in the face. She teetered back and forth before falling. As they gained speed, the tentacle broke loose.

Once they were a safe distance away, they spotted the patrol. Carla slowed down to speak to them.

"Took you long enough!" Liz complained. "There are multiple bodies but don't go now. There is something in the water! Three huge box jellyfish."

One of the guards rolled his eyes. "Like Jaws. You Americans and your horror films. We will take it from here."

The other two guards erupted into laughter as the RIB swerved again and headed towards the catamaran. Guadalupe grabbed the binoculars and scanned the area where the jellies had attacked. They were gone.

Liz tapped away on her laptop, warning everyone she knew on the coast about the threat. The patrol who laughed at them still didn't believe the photos and videos. Carla had shut down her tour side hustle and was advising others to do the same, but with little luck.

Guadalupe pulled away from the microscope and rubbed her eyes. "Whatever this thing is consuming in the garbage is creating this hunger and super-fast growth. What if there are more in other parts of the world? Warmer sea temperatures mean some things will die off and others will thrive."

Guadalupe chewed on the back of her pen as she paced. "There is only one way to kill this thing. We get other creatures to pick it apart and eat it. The main predator for jellyfish are other jellyfish. Birds, green sea turtles, and sharks."

"We throw a buffet beach party for jellyfish and whale sharks?" Liz said. "Sprinkle a little bread to get the gulls?"

"I wish it would be that easy. We need to get into the open water with nets and grab as many man o' wars and jellyfish we can find and lead them to the garbage islands. Then we let nature take its course. You saw how it pursued us. I'm afraid if we get too close it will attack. We could try to torch the islands, but there's no guarantee they won't escape."

"Should I alert the patrol?"

"You saw what they did. No, they will laugh in our faces."

Guadalupe thought for a minute. Then she said, "We go out just before sunlight. The jellyfish will probably be back in hiding. Most of their activity is nocturnal. My guess is it would be best to hit them then. And yes, I'd dump a ton of pellets to attract seagulls.

"We need to make a call to the fisherman to collect as many jellies and man o' wars as they can," Guadalupe continued. "I'll pay them from my own pocket. We don't have time to wait for university approval. Can we get Dillon to make sure the garbage islands haven't moved far from the previous location?"

"I'll message him now," Liz said.

"Why don't I get in touch with the fishermen?" chimed in Carla.

"Thank you. They just fed so it should give us a day or two."

As if blessed by the magic of the gods, the entire operation came together. The fishermen who were struggling were happy to make some fast cash. Dillon patrolled the floating garbage heaps whenever he made a trip out—they moved with the tide but stayed in the same vicinity.

After two days, they had everything they needed. Guadalupe slept maybe four hours the night before going into the water. At 4 a.m. she got out of bed. It was time.

Liz and Carla were waiting for her in front of the hotel. The fishermen had full nets from the previous night and waited not far from the box jelly hiding place. The RIB was already stocked with gull feed.

With no one on the roads, Liz pressed the gas hard. The car screeched into the empty marina parking lot. All three jumped out and rushed to the boat. They changed into wetsuits for safety. No one spoke because the tension had the same stifling pressure as the recent relentless heat.

The sun began to break through striations of milky clouds. The crescent of the moon was still visible. With both the sun and moon in sight she hoped it was a good sign for things to come. Victory.

Carla liked the same speed as Liz. They ploughed through the water. Soon the fishing boats were in view. They began to follow them. Carla backed off as they approached the garbage islands, allowing the fishing boats to unleash their venomous catch. When all the nets were released, Carla circled the islands. The wake pushed the jellyfish closer to the garbage. "Pellet time!" shouted Liz. Both she and Guadalupe dumped sacks upon sacks as Carla still circled. The sun illuminated the water to spun gold. Guadalupe paused to watch daylight crack through the sky fully. Now she knew why all those relationships failed and she had to go to that god-awful church. The things that were meant to be were just dawning.

"Oh my god!" screamed Carla as she stopped the boat.

Two large jellyfish were attempting to climb from the water on top of the garbage heap. Parts of their tentacles were missing and chunks of their hoods. Above their heads the seagulls began to circle. They landed on the islands to pick at the pellets, and then took nips of the jellyfish. Some began to eat the smaller box jellies, carrying them into the sky.

"Fuck, Guadalupe. It's working!"

More seagulls began to feed, and the man o' wars were congregating. Their tentacles pulled at the larger box jellies. Green sea turtles could be seen bobbing to the surface. The two box jellies weren't safe anywhere. Piece by piece, they became consumed by the other creatures of the sea.

Guadalupe hugged Liz. "Thank you."

"No problem. I'm sorry we met in such strange circumstances."

The RIB roared to life. Both Liz and Guadalupe looked at Carla who, though she had turned the boat back on, appeared petrified. They shifted their gaze back to the water. One of the box jellies with a human arm still dissolving in its digestive track had four tentacles on the side of the RIB. Guadalupe looked around for something to fight it off with when another reached out and latched to her ankle. She pulled as hard as she could to escape its grasp. "Go, Carla, shake it off!"

The jelly pulled harder. Carla swerved the boat back and forth while Liz held tight to Guadalupe. "I won't let you fall in!"

Guadalupe could feel the tentacles becoming tighter. The wetsuit was disintegrating. She had brought anti-venom with her, but she hoped it wouldn't come to that.

Liz looked around. "Stop the boat!"

"What? You crazy?" shouted Carla.

"Stop it!"

Carla slowed down. Just as the jelly brought another large tentacle to the side of the RIB, three sharks approached behind it and smashed straight into it. It had no choice but to release its grip. The three women looked back to see more sharks feasting. The heap of garbage was now covered in sea life.

Guadalupe sat on the beach watching the sun set. This time it worked out. But next time they might not be so lucky. She was determined to continue researching the box jellies; next time she would find a way to get a sample of the larger ones. It couldn't be too late to beat the tide of whatever else lurked in the depths devouring waste.

She couldn't stay out late because she was heading to Australia with Liz to study the growing colony of man o' war. The universities of Perth and Lisbon were funding the trip. It also helped that they convinced executives in Japan to chip in once traces of waste were found in the currents surrounding their country, too.

The ocean is huge. There are places that no one had ever ventured into or that could not be ventured into. Now they had to, and they would.

EL ALACRÁN

They call me El Alacrán. The Scorpion. I am the poison of the sea riding on sails of flesh with other women like myself. Our eyes and bodies full of venom, ready to strike at a moment's notice depending on our mood. We stomp across beach after beach in leather boots oiled and dyed crimson from blood. The soles dusty from sand or ash. No loyalty but to each other and no home as most of them were sacked and burned to the ground after one too many wars in rapid succession. We make a living by exploring the fractured world, finding all the hidden treasures from a lost time in history. We took to the sea where there are no borders. No walls nor fences can be placed on something as mighty as the sea. She has no master but herself, her power given to her from the beginning. She is the possessor of life and can be the death of others. We respect her gracious rage. We are pirates.

However, we are not the only ones looking for loot and booty. The small island country of Niaps has risen to unimaginable power with religion and the brutal conquests of desperate territories. The world we sail is one risen from ruin. Many islands were obliterated by war, or all their inhabitants were killed without mercy. The continents had their borders re-carved as survivors created new ways of governing. That was one hundred years ago. Today, we only have remnants of the ages before the wars began. Many, like the women in my family, took to the sea to avoid what happens to women and girls in war. They gave themselves to the sea, and she was good to them. And like in most of the world, the old tech and weaponry that caused all this destruction was discarded. Some was dropped to the depths of the ocean and others blown to bits; however, there was no way of knowing where all of it went or who owned it now. The continents created treaties promising never to use it again. But I'm a pirate. I trust no one but my crew. And I certainly don't trust a piece of paper written by some king in a fortress.

I took a deep inhalation of salty air, particles of sea spray stinging my nostrils and eyes. Dark skies hung low like milk-filled breasts. Soon she would grant us her nourishment to top up our buckets. The deep ocean waters parted for my ship like legs of a welcoming lover. Pleasure and pain of true freedom. I looked to the large mast that holds the sail made from the flayed skins of our vanquished enemies. It caught the wind beautifully. The skin is taken from skeletons with great care, stitched by the younger hands we take under our tutelage on this vessel. The orifices of the nose and mouth patched with the leather or rough cassock of the clothing they wore during their miserable lives. When we approach, the sails look as if they are screaming. Those wails put fear into anyone who might challenge us, lest they become part of our spare sails. Mostly priests and the conquerors who like to call themselves conquistadors on a mission from God and king. They are not messengers from a god, but common thugs with appetites of men. That is why I put no belief in such a deity. I only have faith for my crew, the creatures of the land, the elements, and my instinct. These vicious sails keep us safe.

I take back what I said before. There is only one known god: death. She guides us all through this life.

"Over there, look. They are a good omen. The elements appear to be on our side. So, what's the plan?"

I looked back to Chastity who pointed at the warm water narwhals and dolphins leaping from the waves. My hair whipped against my eyes and mouth. She is the sensible one between us, her hair always in two braids interwoven with red silk. Jade earlobe plugs matched the septum ring through her nose. The color appeared striking against her brown skin, the same shade as my own. The sun made us brown because she knew before we were born it would give us strength as women destined to ride upon the crests of power.

"When do we ever have a plan? How are the new girls doing?"

We both glanced at the recruits still shaken from their ordeal on the island. At least now they had time to go through the booty we took from the conquistadors who snatched whatever they wanted without care. Some of the women cleaned the skulls of their tormentors to be soldered to the ship for decoration. The ship is a tomb of our rage and pain. Conquest comes easy for men, even the small ones. They build worlds that say you cannot exist without them. Diminish yourself until you fit into a satchel they can carry like a coin purse. That is also why we live the way we do. No rules out here.

"They are adjusting. Happy to be around friendly faces."

"Good. Penelope will stay on the ship with them when we reach The Bay of Lost Souls. Any clues about the Skull of Wrath?"

Chastity's eyes sagged when I mentioned the bay. It became renowned for wealth after being plundered and made into a gold refinery and sugar plantation. All the mermaid guardians of the island were slaughtered with barbed fishing nets and cannons bombarding their caves. Not one survived. The calm bay water that usually glittered like a gold coin when the sun sets and rises sloshed against the shore as a rusty lace. Mermaid and human bodies reduced to chum for the creatures of the deep. God, did we make their murderers pay when we landed on shore after receiving word a revolt was planned.

"Cheer up, Chastity. I hear the bay is prettier than ever."

"Hmpf. Until they come back to reclaim their investment with an entire armada."

"That is why we are all meeting."

"I suppose. And no new information on The Skull. Speaking of which, you prepared to see Ossibus?"

My stomach sank with the weight of a shipwreck hearing that name. The last time I saw my mortal enemy, Ossibus, a field of bodies and smoke from flaming arrows separated us as our camps retreated, knowing no one would win this battle. He screamed with a pointed saber in my direction. "El Alacrán! You are a dead woman! I will keep your corpse on my mast so you may not even find rest in the afterlife. You will never escape me." The black abysses of his eyes roiled with contempt and hate.

The remaining flesh on his countenance was smeared with blood, chunks of flesh, and brain matter from those who died from his jagged weapon. A stranger would think he crawled from some abyss because from the nose up, he is only bone. No eyes to see except for the dark magic in his skull that animates him with pure animosity. His lips, jaw, and all the rest is flesh. The seam where skin meets bone is held together by rusty fish hooks. I wonder if he saw the reckless chaos in my eyes because I would let him take my dead body to his ship. Then my immortal soul could torment him night and day. He would want to flee to the conquistador's hell to escape my kiss. But today we must cast those differences aside and join forces against a greater enemy: the conquistadors from the kingdom of Niaps.

It is an island ruled by the same family for centuries. The inbred heirs died, but the ones who survived were afflicted with cruel dispositions. However, just because it was an island did not mean their empire didn't span across other lands under their flag. Their entire army was mostly made up of conquered people. The conquered also had to breed soldiers. Humans born to die. From what I heard from a few of our saved females and a few young males we took elsewhere, there were smaller islands, some called it the Archipelago of Screams because of the constant wailing of females and babies. The strongest of Niaps Armada was stationed there next to a fleet of broken old tech ships. There were great metal beasts of rust making the archipelago difficult to penetrate. On the opposite side were miles of exposed rock and reefs. Sharks patrolled the area feeding off discarded placentas and the corpses of the ones who did not make it.

Those who created such a place and wished to expand it were the real enemy.

Despite the great hatred between Ossibus and I, we are cut from the same cloth. The emissaries from Niaps made it clear by their continual conquests it was complete submission or death. Lies spread to keep the fear suspended like a dead man on a spike. So many fake truths to stoke fear.

"They will lure your husbands into the water and then drain them of their blood."

In fact, the mermaids only ate the vegetation of the sea. No one shed a tear for them when they were murdered, thinking the mermaids were bloodthirsty creatures of the ocean.

"The people of the sea are a scourge. Thieves and rapists. Sea demons. Not even human. No sense of law or order. Illiterate."

I had never raped anyone, only took what was for everyone in the first place, and how can we be illiterate if we can read a map? I read just fine. Wrote a few poems in my day. Can't say if they were any good. But the lies and panic were the true scourge of the mapped-out world slowly being threaded together by the king of Niaps in one great empire under one belief system that upheld his and his cohorts' rule. These thoughts made me as sick as cheap ale did.

In a few hours Ossibus and I would be face to face to join forces. After the last slaughter of the mermaids, we agreed something had to be done. He dropped his sword in the sand, and I dropped mine. It would be only a matter of time before their cannons hunted us. The last of the free people. All our safe havens ports for trade and dealings being patrolled and taken over one by one. We, of course, were not welcome. Riffraff to be exterminated. Not genteel enough, not willing to play their game with their rules knowing they rigged it in their favor.

My heart ached thinking that if Ossibus would be there, so would Antonio. I left him in the night last time with no goodbye. Antonio and I never could stick to being more than occasional tempestuous lovers. We are like the sea and the sky. Although at times they look as if they meet, one and the same, they are separate and occupy different spheres. Both elements have a nature that drives them to always be on the move, ever-changing. He comes from the horn of the mainland Afrik and I Mextique.

As I mentioned, this is about business and survival. I hoped for peace. Love can wait. War is a last resort.

"Ready the anchor!" someone shouted. We had arrived at our destination.

"All right, ladies. As soon as we are off the ship, take her to Whale Cliff. You know the drill when it comes to changing the sails and making us as hidden as possible."

Chastity and I would take a smaller boat to the jetty for the meet. The port had the atmosphere of a burial when we docked. The few souls meandering did so without expression, trying to finish their business before the unseen occurred. The tension of confrontation building. The elements surrounding us vibrated frantically. An ominous wind blew across the jetty. A branch bound to fall from the raging storm. I looked to the thinning clouds blowing in, swirling around the bright sun to form a Mal de Ojo. I whispered to the seagulls flying overhead to carry a message to the sun, *Don't abandon us, as unworthy as we might be. End this fight*, I whispered to the air.

Vendors, children, even the beggars made themselves scarce. It had been so very long since this many pirates had gathered in one place. Usually we scuffled with each other, today we put all things aside to unite. Show our force and take a stand. Tolerance and peace, or everyone suffers in a battle of constant tit for tat.

"You ready?"

I broke my gaze and nodded my head. To ensure everyone we meant no harm, or to refresh our sails made from flesh, it would be just Chastity and I to represent our crew.

The village had the same stifled atmosphere as the port. No one sweeping the front of their home, selling food or their wares. Huts remained shut. I suspected a few of the villagers left for the forest to wait out our meeting. The only sound came from the inn where many would gather. Laughter. I exhaled a deep breath hearing jovial voices as opposed to fighting. The price too high for us to fight amongst ourselves.

The stench of ale, bad breath, freshly baked bread, and unwashed bodies hit my nostrils as I walked in. We had all sailed as quickly as we could to make it here in time. No time for rest or baths. Antonio stood at the front of the inn with Ossibus by his side. They are brothers by blood after all. His crew across three ships consisted of forgotten humans cut from all different color and texture of fabrics, creatures who were half human and half otherworldly that defied explanation. Some were neither female nor male. Together they found a home with Ossibus and Antonio. The pirate life included everyone. The sea claimed lives and gave bounty blindly. The ones on the run needed leaders to find sanctuary after being driven out by the human hordes, reviled for being 'demons.'

Antonio met my eyes. His gaze always left me feeling landlocked. He gave me a nod before scanning the crowd to tally if the major crews were represented. Mine had to be the last to arrive by the look of the crowd.

He pushed towards the bar and yanked hard on a brass bell. That man hailed from royalty, and it showed when he spoke in front of a crowd. "Thank you all for coming We are here to discuss the raids by priests and conquistadors. They call us no good sea demons, but in truth they are more ruthless. I heard they melted down the antiquities found on the mainland of Afrik. Made an image of the king instead. This very bay sliced by their sword. We are not perfect. A few of you downright scoundrels I wouldn't trust the rats on my ship with, but the big is we all sail for ourselves whereas they are united under one flag. My brother Ossibus has found a way to finally bring their king to the table."

Never one to let the men have all the say, I had to speak up. "Will it involve magic? It will just prove to those land devils that we are savages in need of their god. It will make things worse. If we need his forces, okay. No magic. Sorry, Ossibus."

Ossibus stepped towards me. His skin as flawless as the exposed skull on the top of his head. "It is through magic I have brought us all good fortune and a gift."

He flicked his head to someone in the back. The crowd whispered to themselves, taking sips of their ale and wine.

One of the female pirates from Antonio's crew escorted another woman from the back of the inn. Her hands were bound with rope. She had to be royalty. Royalty from our enemies. The dress she wore appeared tattered from the voyage. The delicate silks and lace stained and ripped. The necklace with bright jewels surrounding a gold crest remained on her neck. Her hair was as black as mine, her eyes the color of a flawless emerald. Her skin would be the same as mine if allowed in the sun. Ossibus had brought us a queen. *The Queen of Niaps*.

"So, Ossibus, I guess you want the armada to land and destroy us. No wonder the village emptied out.

"We emptied the village. They wait in the forest. She is a tool to get the king of Niaps to talk. The corridors of trade are narrowing. Whenever any of us send out messengers, they don't return, or only parts of them return."

I looked to the queen. Maybe he was right. We approached the wrong person. "Why do you kill us?"

"We don't want to kill you. You force us. Just submit. Bow to the crown. There are rules for each territory to follow. Just do what is asked of you."

"Don't give me any of your fancy political talk. What is coming next and how can we stop it?"

She bit her cracked lip and looked at me with her weary seagrass green eyes. "Don't you see, you can't stop it. History is being written and nothing will ever be the same again. I am the only reason my country survived. A gem of clean blood to purify the inbred Niaps bloodline. It can't be stopped. No matter how many battles you wage, they cannot overwhelm the united mainland desire for destiny. Their power . . . their firepower that has been stockpiled. Our people believe in their king and god as one, even if it is not so. You fight a losing battle."

She attempted to adjust her corset which looked uncomfortable. The whalebone sticking into her ribs, no doubt. "Would you like some privacy to change? I have clothes you can wear. Then I want to hear about this stockpiled artillery."

"No, I'm fine. I was born into it. It is all that has been expected of me. Besides, my King will be here soon."

In her eyes I saw the truth. It was destiny. There were more mainlands and people on those mainlands than us on the seas. The people of the islands living their lives, not expecting or equipped to deal with this kind of cunning cruelty. The mermaids knew. This captive was no threat at this moment, so I untied her hands.

A boy ran into the inn, out of breath. His cheeks red. "We have incomers."

My head whipped back to the queen. Her gaze looked far beyond us. "He is here."

"He must love you a hell of a lot."

"He loves glory. I'm a means to an end. And he no longer has love for me. I have lost every child we have conceived. No one can tell me why. All of the procedures have failed."

I motioned for her to come with me, but not before giving her another drink of water from the horn goblet with a hoof at the bottom. Chastity and I led her to the back of the inn.

"Maybe you are not destined to be a mother of an heir. There are other places in this world for us. And maybe he shouldn't have an heir."

She raised her head slightly with tears in her eyes. Finery doesn't mean freedom if it's not your own.

"Wait here. You won't be harmed. I promise."

She nodded, still expressionless and slightly dazed. I had the impression that she didn't care if she lived or died. When I entered the front room, the king of Niaps sat at the table. His face calm, clear. Not a worry, like a god on a throne that fears nothing because he has seen the past, present, and future. He looked across the room with jewel-colored eyes that matched the rings on his fingers. His clothing all leather with only a solid gold collar with a crest in the center. It was a hound with an open mouth and bared fangs. His clasped hands rested on the table. Not a callous or sun burn. No marks but soft skin soaked in milk, no doubt. Or the blood of virgins.

"You have my wife. You are on my land. I respectfully ask for her back and you to submit to your king."

"We have not harmed your queen. Sirena can vouch for that." Antonio stretched out his hand towards me. "And it is you who forced our hand. Your priests and conquistadors are roaming the mapped world unchecked. By any means necessary you are trying to get every sovereign territory left under your banner. You can no longer deny that magic exists. Your priests want to obliterate any signs of it, but this is impossible. Maybe it is you who needs to submit to what the world is really like."

The king looked unmoved by Antonio. "Why should I accept a world as it is when I can mold it to whatever I want it to be?" He turned his attention to me. "Thank you, my dear handmaiden, for taking care of my beautiful wife. You may leave now."

I stepped closer and sat on the table, one leg on the floor while the other dangled in the air. I made sure to lean in so he could see I cared less if he caught a slight sight of my breast. Things men desire to ravage at will, yet I'm told to hide. "I am no handmaiden or vestal virgin, dear king. I am part of this pirate horde as you so respectfully call us. Not going anywhere."

"But you are a . . ."

"I'm a what? A savage? Barbarian. True." I flashed him the most defiant smile I could muster.

"You're a woman."

"Really? I am? Thank you for that knowledge. Your god truly has blessed you with such a gift of observation. I wonder what you would be like if you were blessed with magic?"

"Sirena," Ossibus growled.

I rose from the table and stood next to Antonio with arms crossed and my gaze fixed on the king. "Say what you need to say. We already have our terms, but since you are a guest on the island, you can go first."

He blinked his eyes as if he had woken from a pleasant nap. It made me suspicious. This was not a look of impending negotiation. This was the smug look of a winning hand.

"Thank you for bringing me here and showing me your faces. I have underestimated you, but you have underestimated me. As we speak, the forest is being lit with fire. Give me my queen and surrender this island, or I torch the entire place."

Then we heard it. The sound could have been from a dragon if dragons existed. The queen was right, but our conversation had been interrupted before she could tell us everything, The room filled with the roar of forbidden technology. The simple wooden furniture shook violently from the force generated from the propulsion system. Glass bottles shattered on the floor. Us pirates looked around the room in fear and awe. Swords and knives unsheathed for a threat we could not possibly overwhelm. We had heard the tales.

You see, our ancestors suffered and witnessed an end to civilization. To right all the wrongs, technology was no longer created or used. All of it destroyed to start from zero. Species on the brink of extinction flourished. The creatures of the dark emerged from their shadows to live among humans. We also rediscovered ancestral magic. It didn't take many generations for old patterns to take hold over the planet. Now this king used forbidden technology to destroy us. He had been using it all along.

Soldiers wearing gray metal suits and helmets stormed through the doors. This was not the flimsy armor worn by the conquistadors. This was fire- and probably cannon-resistant. They pointed weapons at us that would cut us down in seconds. Our steel was useless. You need to be in a certain range to kill with a blade. By the time we made it close enough to use our steel, a pulse of heat would fill our bellies or chests. We huddled in the corner poised to fight a lost battle. The soldier without a helmet or metal armor stood next to the king. He appeared to be from my mainland with the same dusty shade of skin as my own. A tattoo behind his ear thee same as some of the men wore when they finished their studies. His earlobe plugs removed, but the stretched skin showed he once wore them.

"Lobo, find my queen and bring her here."

My first thought was of Chastity who was with the queen. Some luck had to spare her. Fear shook my internal organs to the point of self-combustion. I looked to Ossibus who was itching for a fight. He snarled with one hand on his saber. A saber that would not withstand the weapons the soldiers carried. He knew this. I could see this knowledge smouldering in his skull. Antonio met my eyes. Unlike his brother, I only saw defeat and sadness within him. This strange turn of events was worse than any of us imagined. The king had been waiting for the perfect opportunity to unveil his plan. You can change the structure of civilization, but it is nothing unless you change the inclination of heart and mind. The ones who refuse to sacrifice heart and mind willingly are made examples of. The villages and ports we entered never mentioned this technology. The soldier returned with the queen at his side. She walked in with a dreamy look on her face, and then sorrow as her eyes met her husband. She'd known all along. She saved her people from this very threat by offering her body to produce an heir and name.

The king scarcely glanced at the queen. "Wonderful. Now take those three." The king extended a soft limp finger to Ossibus, Antonio, and I."

"What? My king?" Cassandra pleaded.

He turned on his heels with the man he called Lobo. He leaned in and whispered something to him. Lobo nodded before glancing back at a cluster of soldiers. "Take those three and the queen to the hovercraft."

I looked to the queen who had tears streaming from her eyes. She didn't resist five soldiers leading us out of the inn. Our weapons taken from us with the point of their weapons to our heads. I didn't want to look back at the inn. The last thing I heard was the clattering of steel falling to the floor and the soldiers spilling forth. "Lock the inn and we will take it out from above." My heart said a silent prayer for all of them as we stepped onto the open metallic mouth of the hovercraft. *Chastity!* I screamed in my mind. I wanted to kill them all with my bare hands and teeth if need be. As we entered the hovercraft door slammed shut. The soldiers surrounded us, but my attention was not on them. Despite the fear, I felt in awe of this ship I had only heard stories about. Lights blinked not from magic or fire. Everything made from metal. The science of destruction never left the world. I could feel us rising off the ground. Antonio grabbed the crook of my elbow as we rose.

"Stand there." The soldier appeared just as scared of us as we were of him with his foreign weapon. He had the look of a kid with only soft down above his lip. Probably pulled from the countryside and promised the world if he risked his life for king and empire. Six soldiers rounded us in the center of the craft. The queen stood behind me. Her fingertips brushed against mine. "Your friend. I told her to hide when I heard the king's voice. We can only hope she made it out after I left."

This whisper felt like a break in a storm. I exhaled deeply and bowed my head to say a prayer to the universe to spare Chastity and everyone on the island. My eyes caught something else.

We stood in a square, like a seam. A hatch. This couldn't be good. My mind didn't know if this meant anything because the queen stood with us as well. Maybe the sense of unease was only my paranoia as a pirate. I still braced. I elbowed Ossibus and Antonio with the slyness only a female knows and then darted my eyes so they could see what I saw. Ossibus nodded and then glanced at Antonio. "We need to be ready for anything," Antonio whispered.

We flew for what felt like minutes. Before we had any time to react, we heard a mechanical whir followed by the sensation of free fall. The blessed ocean air carried my hair above my head. They were sending us straight into the ocean. The crash was less painful than what I had imagined. Couldn't have been too high. My eyes popped open so I might see the ocean and she could see me. Perhaps the ocean would spare her friend.

I watched both Ossibus and Cassandra slip into the cold murkiness of the vast ocean. Cassandra's heavy dress billowed around her body like the bulbous body of a jellyfish. Her long hair and arms swayed as freely as tentacles. In her wide eyes I could see not in a million years did she imagine her life would end like this. Ossibus sank to his end next to her in the same manner as he had lived his life. He fought against the water. Veins bulged from the sides of his neck. Eyes bugged out, hating the water's existence when really, the water did nothing but be what it was. From my peripheral vision, I saw scales. A mermaid lifted her index finger to me as she took one of my hands. I could only save one. In my mind I prayed for a miracle. Would the bubbles escaping my nose and mouth carry my pleas? Not what I usually did. Not my nature hardened by the nature of this world. I reached for Ossibus. I knew from Antonio that they were not extended many hands in their lives. I'd save my enemy in hope this would earn back a little of my grace for my journey if I survived. As much as I wanted to save Cassandra, I knew her loyalty would have to be to her husband. Disloyalty to him would end in her death. Unlike me, she was not her own woman.

Then, as if the water could hear my thoughts and sent out a call, two more mermaids appeared, swimming hard against the current with a pink dolphin. The dolphin pushed Cassandra towards the surface. The two mermaids aided the one pulling me up by the arm. Ossibus surrendered to their help. His eyes caught my heavy gaze. The flames in his skull lit slightly. In the black pits where eyes used to reside, he gave me an apology. He accepted my hand. He is too proud to ever thank me with his voice. I accepted his flame as acknowledgement.

We broke through the surface. The night was ablaze from the destruction reflected on the water's surface. It appeared as if the entire world was burning. All our sins and hate consuming us in fire. One we lit.

The mermaids pulled us to a cove. Without a word they dove back under to avoid danger. Cassandra heaved in her dripping corset. A soft sob escaped her lips. Ossibus sat upright with his head hanging between his knees, clutching the spot where his precious saber once hung. My chest burned from choking on saltwater. Saliva and snot covered my face. Had Antonio received help from the sea? Watching the fire coming from the village brightened something inside of me, a fury I had not felt since I left for the seas at nineteen. I had to find a way to broker peace. We couldn't live like this. No one would survive. Not a soul at this rate. The killing enough to steal what was left of our souls.

Ossibus reared his head towards me. "So, what do we do now?"

I looked to the sky to see a large aircraft with the king's crest on the side leaving. We wouldn't have long to look for survivors or gather ourselves. The conquistadors from this empire always operated the same way. Slash and burn, and then leave. They returned when the people were so desperate they would accept any scraps thrown their way.

"We regroup our friends," I said. "Help the villagers as much as we can. Then we sail to find a way to end this. I have an idea, but that will be for later. No time for tears."

Ossibus stood and extended a hand to the queen. "You will not be harmed, but you will receive no special treatment."

"I will tell you everything I know." She took his hand and rose from the sand, trying not to stare at his face. I inhaled a deep breath before getting to my feet, not fully knowing what to think about our narrow escape. Even if we didn't have technology, we had the power and magic of the natural world. I didn't want to be cruel; however, I had to let Cassandra know where she stood under our protection.

"You will need to prove you can be trusted. I don't know your people. All I know is what your husband has done over the last few years."

"Sirena is right," Ossibus said. "The king has done nothing but collect sovereign territories like gold coins. You have everything to gain by staying with him. Pirates stick to our own . . . if . . ."

A large boom filled the atmosphere followed by a tsunami of sand hitting us all, causing a moment of blindness and coughing.

"Scorpion! El Alacrán! You need to know when it's time to die."

I whipped my head towards Ossibus. "Get her out of here now. Whatever she knows about Niaps we need. You know my secrets when it comes to backup plans."

He gave me a short nod before running with his hand around Cassandra's wrist.

I turned back to the gritty cloud of sand settling back to the ground. There stood Lobo with one of his old tech weapons in hand. His feet barely touched the ground with the help of some sort steel box on his back. Fucking tech. I had to live to tell this tale because we were facing weaponry long gone. He could fly.

When his feet touched the sand, he stepped closer to me with a smug grin. He enjoyed feeling superior in this moment.

"What are you waiting for? Your fire power is faster than my steel."

He gave me a bitter smirk. "I know. It's amusing to see you trying to understand what is to come. Great gear, eh? Get ready to die from it."

With his right hand, he raised his weapon and fired. In those few seconds I had to move from his crosshairs, the weapon stalled. I was already laying on the sand and kicking more his way when the weapon fired.

"I hate these places!" he screamed. When he landed, his weapon must have taken sand into the barrel, disrupting the laser.

"Why? Because the sand gets into everything?"

I swiped across his femur the gold dagger I kept in a gold sheaf beneath whatever I wore on a band of leather strapped around my ribcage.

He screamed out in pain from the small wound before his body began to convulse. This dagger is in a metal sheath because the tip is always dripping with poison.

I grabbed his weapon and knelt next to him. "I know you aren't here alone. Tell me where the others are and I will give you the antidote."

He let out a violent cough that left a pool of blood in the sand. To encourage him I showed him a leather pouch around my neck. "It's right here."

His eyes rolled back before fixing on the pouch. "Fine. In the forest. It's a small airship. Only two others. The larger ship is long gone. But it will be back."

"Thank you. And I'm sorry to tell you that there is nothing in this pouch but a seashell. You will be the one to die a slow death now, like so many I have seen with the Niaps conquest."

He growled and coughed through gritted teeth as I rose from the sand to catch up with the others. There was no time if I was to meet Ossibus. My thighs ached from running hard through the dunes, but I couldn't curse the sand too much. It had just saved my skin.

Then in the distance I could see my beloved flesh sails. My crew was looking to the shore to find me. And to my surprise, Ossibus waited on the beach with sword and spyglass in hand. He tucked the spyglass under his woven cloth belt before running towards me. The crew jumped off the boat one by one once they saw it was safe.

Cassandra ran towards me with a waterskin. I needed it. Without caring if it made my shirt translucent, I drank with greed, allowing the water to splash and fall from my mouth.

"How did you do it?"

Ossibus smirked. "She is called El Alacrán . . . she deals in poison. She is the poison."

I lifted my shirt to the side to reveal the leather holster.

"I keep this blade dipped in venom from the deadliest jellyfish in the sea."

"Ossibus, you and I have business in the forest. Before Lobo kicked the bucket, he told me two others waited for him. But what should we do with her?"

Cassandra shifted her gaze between Ossibus and I.

"I promise I can be trusted."

Ossibus cocked his head towards the ship. "Chastity can handle it."

I looked around the beach. "She's here? She made it?"

"Of course, you are all a tough lot. She's on the ship."

My heart lifted. Maybe this would be okay in the end. I had to appreciate the small wins. And if I was honest, it was nice to have a partner like Ossibus. He wasn't as flaky as Antonio. Chastity could manage the crew while we finished the battle. And Ossibus and I knew battle well.

We walked through the decimated village. The tavern we had sat and drank in hours before still smoked. Charred bodies of humans and animals crumbled before our eyes. Young and old were executed without mercy. No one was spared. I swallowed hard because my tears and pain wanted to erupt into wrath. I was the Skull of Wrath wanting the blood of those who had innocent blood on their hands. Old tech was still lethal and precise. No wonder so many fought hard to get it banned. We would have ended up blowing up the entire planet. I didn't want any part of it in whatever territories we kept safe. I looked over at Ossibus; he could not cry, but the flames that were usually a violet blue were bright orange. The top of his skull glowed from the fire.

"I hate seeing this, Ossibus, but it keeps my blood boiling to never stop."

Ossibus kicked a stone broken off from the blasted walls of a house. "Same. We will be unstoppable when it comes to vengeance and hunting down the king."

"You tried. How were we to know how much tech they had? The villagers didn't stand a chance."

He stopped and looked at me. The bright fire eased down to the violet blue again. "Thank you, Sirena."

I didn't want to get too emotional, so I just flashed a soft smile before continuing to walk. The forest wasn't far from the village once we passed the last of the larger houses. I glanced at Ossibus to see if he was ready. "Nice saber."

"Yeah, Chastity said it was your spare. Not bad. It feels good in hand. And looks like you have something new."

"It was Lobo's. The sand jammed it when he fired. I'll try it out and if it doesn't work, well, I'll have to take that back."

As we neared the tree line we could hear voices. It had to be the two soldiers Lobo had told me about. We crept quietly watching our steps. I wasn't sure about this weapon and how to take correct aim. I'd wait until we were close and I knew I wouldn't miss. Neither could escape. The ship would have to be destroyed because tech like this was probably tracked. Ossibus jerked his head towards the back of the ship. I knew what he was doing. It was easy to anticipate his moves. He raised his saber and I the weapon. I mouthed, *NOW.*

We rushed behind them before they had a chance to turn around and grab their weapons. Ossibus raised the saber and drove it through the center of one of their skulls. The power of his hit cracked the soldier's cranium like a coconut. Flakes of bone and blood escaped the wound. At the same time, I aimed the weapon and pressed the top of it with my thumb the way Lobo did. A large hole blasted through the other soldier's chest.

"No witnesses to go running to the king. We can breathe a little easier now that we can regroup. I'll send a few of the crew to come take this thing apart. Maybe we can use parts. Who knows."

Ossibus was admiring my saber. "You got good steel, Sirena. It is an honor to now fight by your side. Let's go plan the next phase."

My fingertips ran across the helm of my ship, thinking of Antonio because it felt so comfortable with Ossibus. You can't float a boat made from leather and fine lace, as beautiful as it might be. I'm okay not belonging to anyone. Wounds I won't have to mend.

I looked to the mast with the sails made from vanquished enemies. Flesh will not scare the ones possessing technology. Then a wisp of a cloud in the shape of feathers, perhaps wings, passed overhead. I forgot my own desires and turned my gaze to the horizon. When I feel the need to cry, I stand on the deck in the rain. No one can tell the difference between sea spray from rough seas, rain, or my tears. We will keep sailing.

"Sirena."

I turned to see Ossibus standing next to me. He is the first man to be on one of my ships and allowed to live.

"What now? Please don't tell me we have someone on our tail. I think I need a short rest before I get into another fight."

He looked out to the sea. "You're telling me the indominable scorpion is low on venom?"

I couldn't help but chuckle. "Okay, then. Speak your piece."

He took a deep breath and looked directly at me. "I'm not like my brother. I hate words and don't have many. I'm not charming or good looking. My instinct is to destroy anyone who crosses me."

"Tell me something I don't know, Ossibus. And you know I am kinda the same."

"I'm sorry, and thank you."

This was very unexpected. "It only took me saving your life for you to realize our dispute was your fault?"

"And when we both tried to get the same thing, we both lost it."

There was an awkward silence we allowed the ocean to ameliorate. When you love the sea, the waves more times than not can do the speaking for you, or at least bind wind-whipped thoughts.

"Maybe . . ."

Ossibus had something big he wanted to say. I knew it was important because of the way he fiddled with the railing of the boat.

"Yes . . ."

"Maybe we should find the Skull of Wrath together?"

Perhaps his near-death experience had changed something inside of him.

"So you can use me to get it and then kill me? No, thanks. I like my skin . . ."

"No. This is bigger than us. I like my skin, too, but I won't have it for long if Niaps makes the entire world their empire. No, thanks."

I had to think on this. It was a good proposal. At the same moment, we turned to each other.

"Together we could be . . ."

I took a step back. "You go first. We could be what?"

"Unstoppable."

"My venom and your magic."

"Yes."

"Why didn't we do this before instead of fighting?"

"Sometimes we have to fight lessons before we surrender and learn from them."

This was a side to Ossibus I had never seen. It made me think of what had started our feud to begin with.

The Skull of Wrath. It was the prize everyone who sailed the seas sought to possess. Legend said it was the skull of a demon summoned by the mermaids to fend off the humans who attacked them. But the demon escaped and began to destroy the seabed. With the help of pirates, the mermaids caught the demon and destroyed it. The skull is said to possess whoever stares into its dark sockets. The possessed will be taken to madness and destroy themselves.

It had the power to destroy an enemy with one glance and without raising a single sword. Whisper in its ear and it will destroy whoever you wish.

I wanted the Skull of Wrath because the mermaids had begged me to destroy it.

Ossibus, I assumed, wanted it for his own use. Now, if we could have it in our hands, we could use it against the king. Then I would destroy it.

The fight between Ossibus and I began when I was with his brother Antonio. It was late and more than a few drinks in. The following morning I was sailing to find the skull. Until that point, I'd told no one.

"I wish you could stay." Antonio kissed me on the neck as he brushed my hair away. Ossibus alone looked on. I always thought his half human, half bone face was sexy. Back then we were all just out of our teen years. He should have been having fun, yet he was so serious.

"Where you off to, Sirena?"

I pushed Antonio away before glancing around the room.

"The Skull of Wrath," I said in a low tone.

Antonio laughed so loud I had to elbow him. "Now that is a story."

Both Ossibus and I looked at him and said at the same time. "No, it's not."

We looked at each other again. The flames in his eyes were brighter than before.

"The Skull is mine," Ossibus said. "I've been searching for it for years. What are *you* going to do with it?"

"What are you going to do with it? I know you have a small band of riffraff sea rats who idolize you and follow you around."

Ossibus stood up, knocking our horns of alcohol across the table. "That is none of your business."

I stood to match his gaze and stance. "Well, my desire for it is none of yours either."

We were two young hot heads thinking we were the best at sea.

Antonio merely waved over the tavern maid for another drink.

"We will see, Sirena, who can find it first. I will be damned if you think I would let you have it. It's . . . important for me."

"It's important for me, too. I have others counting on me to find it."

"Aha! You are going to get paid!"

I unsheathed my dagger. "You'll never see it."

Ossibus flipped the table, "Anyone who is with me leaves now. We have waves to catch and a skull to find. Maybe crush a few."

He stormed out with a dozen others trailing behind him. I looked at Antonio. "What do you know about your brother?"

"I don't know. He is so damn serious . . . like you. I'm surprised you don't get along better."

He hadn't noticed anything that had just occurred as he was busy checking out the tavern maid who was making eyes at him. But that was Antonio. It was my time to hit the sea.

"Catch you later, Antonio."

"Uh, yes. See you soon."

He had already forgotten I was leaving. And he didn't care. I'd let my crew sleep tonight, but I would sleep alone on my ship. She never let me down and I had a skull to chase.

For the next ten years, Ossibus and I were hot on each other's heels between other adventures and small battles. Ossibus was my male counterpart in the sea.

"Not interested?

"Sorry, Ossibus. I was just thinking about how our feud began. Has it really been ten years? But I am very interested."

He smiled with the flames flickering in his sockets and then snapped it back. "There is something I really need to know. Who hired you to find The Skull?"

"No one hired me. The mermaids begged me find it and destroy it. And you?"

Ossibus threw his head back and shook it. His skull glowed from the fire inside.

"For ten years we have been at each other's throats, almost killing one another for the same thing. They asked me as well."

I touched his arm. "Why didn't you say anything?"

Briefly, he looked at my hand before I brought it back. "I told you I was not a talker, Sirena."

His softer tone made me soften mine. "You have real love for the mermaids, don't you?"

"Yes, one of them saved me when I was a very young man. It made me look like this, but at least I am alive and Antonio and our mother survived."

Ossibus

The stormy waters were far from safe; however, staying in the village was even more lethal. The cannons fired without any discrimination. Antonio and his brother Azul were five and six. Their mother tried to hold on tight to both of them, containing her own fear. She whispered to the sea for salvation and protection. A large splash hit the three of them. The cold made her take a deep breath with the boat rocking side to side. She looked around to see if her children were all right.

Antonio was there. Azul waved his arms trying to find his way back to his mother, but there was no way to fight the sea.

Not knowing how to escape the current, he slipped under. Then tender hands scooped him up, and he breathed oxygen distilled from her gills into his mouth until they reached the surface of the water. The mermaid waded until she could see the small boat. She beat her tail hard to reach the side.

"Your child."

The woman clutched her chest. "I thought I lost him forever. Thank you."

"He is innocent and should be protected. Here, in the event he ever needs anything else from the sea." The mermaid removed a braided seaweed necklace from around her neck with a coral pendant carved in the shape of a star.

With a trembling hand the woman took the necklace and placed it on Azul's neck. His eyes fluttered. Before the woman could say another word, the mermaid was gone.

The small family made it across the strait without further bombing. The hideous attack focused solely on the village to raze it to the ground. Anais watched as her livelihood and life burned to nothing. But she had her family.

Eleven years later it wasn't soldiers they had to worry about: it was the raiders. And they arrived with only killing and gold on their minds.

"Don't fight with me, Antonio. Get her out of here. The boat is ready with supplies."

"What about you? You can't expect me to leave you behind."

Azul had his sword in hand. Sweat rolled down his face as the shouts of the raiders and screams of fishermen became louder.

"Don't leave us, Azul!" screamed Anais.

Azul shook his head. "Never. I will be back."

Before Antonio could stop him, Azul ran to the ensuing skirmish between villagers and raiders. He had made money collecting debts or providing protection to rich travellers. Battles were not common. He hoped his training was enough.

The battle was lost when two of them held his arms to his side. The raider's blade glinted in the relentless sun, and it was that time of year when the sun didn't set until midnight.

"All you peasants are the same. You fight for next to nothing in these nothing villages, and perhaps that is why you fight to the death. It will bring you closer to ending your misery!"

The raider's black and brown gums looked hideous, almost inhuman with his two canines pointed and other teeth missing.

"Do what you want. I won't beg," spat Azul.

The raider leaned closer. Hairs from his nose and eyebrows shot out in all directions as he growled, "Then you won't mind what I'm about to do."

Azul wouldn't beg for his life, but he couldn't stop from screaming as the raider gouged out each eye from his skull. Blood ran down his cheeks instead of tears.

Just as the shock from the pain set in, another searing pain pulled at his senses. The crowd of raiders hooted and howled as a blade ran across the top half of his head.

"I'm keeping the rest of your ugly mug so you can keep screaming."

He said this while removing the flesh clean from his skull. Azul's entire body tensed as he braced against the pain. His shirt torn from the fight dripped with sweat and blood. As the raider ripped off the remaining flesh with the precision of peeling a fruit, Azul collapsed.

The next thing he remembered was a frigid blanket surrounding him and water filling his lungs. Flashes of his childhood cratered his mind. With what little strength he had left in his body, he clutched the piece of coral and hardened seaweed on his neck. He hoped his mother and brother at least had enough time to escape.

That is when his body regained a sense of buoyancy. He couldn't see, only feel. The water was less cold. And then it all went black.

"Wake up. You must wake up or sleep forever. Open your eyes."

Azul groaned. "How can I open my eyes when they took them . . . and my flesh."

"Only a blind man thinks the only way to see is through flesh." And then: "Do you want to see?"

Azul remained silent.

He could feel a wet, scaly slap against his body. "I said do you want to see?"

"Yes!" he roared.

Within seconds the world was bright again. In fact, it was brighter than before with a kaleidoscope of colors.

"How . . ."

He looked around to find himself in a cave. The water gently lapped the shore where he lay next to a fire. A mermaid sat half in and half out of the soft waves.

"Magic of the sea. But I must warn you that you do not appear as you did before. We did the best we could."

Azul sat upright with pain shooting the length of his sore body. "I don't care. I'm alive and I can see my family again."

"They are fine. The most important thing is that you allow yourself to heal and become accustomed to this new version of yourself."

Slowly, Azul brought his fingers to his chin and began to inch his way up. Metal. He moved his fingers further up his skull. Bone. As he reached his eye sockets there was heat. He snapped his fingers back.

"What is this?"

The mermaid handed him a polished oyster shell. Azul took it into his hand and took a deep breath. Waiting wouldn't make it easier.

The flesh from the bottom half of his face was attached to bone with fish hooks. The rest of his face was pure white skull. In his eye sockets flared two flames.

"Your sight is from a volcanic sea vent where lava escapes from the depths of our world. The flames themselves are from the lava. Your flesh would eventually rot and shrivel away so we kept it attached with enchanted hooks.

He continued to stare at his face. "Thank you for saving me. What I look like doesn't matter. My face would end up wrinkled and rot away anyhow."

"You'll retain your youth longer now, if that gives you any comfort."

Azul attempted to stand but had no strength in his body.

"I wouldn't. The magic is strong. You must be here until the new moon. I will bring you fish to build your strength, and then you can go. Azul, do not fear for your future. You have more power from this transformation than you could ever imagine. But there is a mission we will have in the future for you. A skull you will need to find."

"Let me start with changing my name. I am Ossibus."

Ossibus and I watched the waves for a while before Cassandra joined us. She now wore a simple cotton blouse and trousers with sturdy boots like the rest of the women we took in. "Where are we going?"

"We are going to find our own weapon. It's a skull. We want to use it against the king and then destroy it."

"Tell me what I can do to help."

Ossibus gave her a wide grin. "Oh, you will help. You have to tell us how to get close to him."

"Anything."

"And I have a question for you," I said. "If you were on the throne, what would you do? Or would someone from your family take it from you?

Cassandra looked to the sea. Her already brown skin was taking on a deeper shade. "Who says I would want the throne? I've seen what it has done to those in my family and the husband who was never really my husband."

"And you?" Cassandra asked. "You are strong-willed and smart. You know how to lead."

"No, thanks, I like my freedom on the sea," I said. "The details of ruling should be left for the ones responsibly bred for it. Magic is more interesting than bureaucracy. It's time we talk magic and unfortunately we don't have much time. We should go below deck and come up with a plan. Cassandra, I want you to help the others with repairing boots and drying fish."

"I have never done that before, but I will do my best."

"Good. A fine lady knows how to do many things." I sat at the table with Ossibus and Chastity. "So, you tell us the last trail that led to the whereabouts of the Skull of Wrath. We ran out of clues."

Ossibus stood and took off his shirt. I had to stop myself from looking too hard out of admiration. He had the night sky tattooed on his chest along with scars from battle. He turned around to show us his back. When I knew he couldn't see me, I slyly looked to Chastity with wide eyes and mouthed, *Wow.*

His back had just as many scars but also names of different ports and seas. There was a final one. *Corteza Bay.*

"What are we looking at here besides you showing off?"

"All the leads I have followed that led nowhere. This is the last, and I hope the right one."

I glanced back at Chastity. "You know it?"

She stood. "I do. I'll change course."

Chastity left us to prepare the crew.

"Thank you, Ossibus. You have had so many more leads than us. We dock and spend a few days looking around without luck. But when it's close, I will know."

He turned to face me. "How? Even I don't have that power."

I took the leather pouch around my neck from beneath my shirt. "This. The mermaids said . . ."

My eyes couldn't help to scan his bare chest again.

"Yes."

"They said I would be pulled towards the location like the tide with the moon. I would see the location before I felt it. In the end, all is hidden in plain sight."

"That's strange because I was told the same beginning and end as that riddle, but the middle was that I had to accept the hand that would pull me close . . . You. I accepted your help when I was drowning. And now it seems we both have what is needed to complete the mission."

There had always been this magnetism between us. It was more than hate; the opposite, perhaps.

"I guess we are bound until the task is done."

He grabbed his shirt. "I could think of worse partners."

I couldn't help but smile at him and the flashing blue-violet flames in the sockets of his skull.

"Same. Now, let's have a drink while we float to our destiny."

Corteza Bay was one of the last untouched territories. It was protected by tribes who lived in the thick jungle. But who knows how long that would last with the old tech coming back. Would they torch the entire swatch of lush forest? Nothing was impossible with the king of Niaps. As soon as we approached, I touched the leather pouch and took out the small white and pink clamshell inside. It wasn't anything special. There were more magnificent ones in the vast waters; however, the mermaids gave this one all the magic I needed to find the skull. Now the location was right in front of me.

My sternum tingled as we entered the shallows where we would have to anchor. "Ossibus, feel this."

I took his hand and placed it over the pouch on my chest. He stood close to me. "Your heart is racing, but my hand . . . It's vibrating. There's heat. I feel it."

All I could do was nod. "Your location was correct and now my shell is saying we are at the right place at the right time."

"We will dock soon. You two ready?"

Ossibus retracted his hand quickly upon hearing Chastity's voice. He attempted to sound gruff. "All I need is my saber . . . I mean, Sirena's saber I'm borrowing."

Chastity giggled when he walked away.

"What?" I playfully swatted her with a piece of rope tied to the mast.

"You two go from literally trying to kill and outsmart each other to passionate soulmate sex . . . What about Antonio? I support whatever you choose."

"Antonio will find a bed to keep warm. He always does. And what sex? It's been as dry as a sandbar."

"And destiny waits for no one, right?" she said with a large grin.

"Nope. Our boots stay bloody no matter what."

It was late afternoon and my chest felt unrelentingly tight. I knew it was here. This was the place. Whispers about the king of Niaps getting closer plagued every tavern and stall we passed. Ossibus and I kept to ourselves as we wandered for hours looking for clues.

When the stalls began to pack up, we decided to head back to the ship. It was time to eat supper. On the jetty I had to stop. In front of a small boat was a young woman with her father. She looked hopeful, whereas exhaustion had taken his hair and dried his flesh. On the ground she sat with dried eels, strands of braided seaweed, and an opalescent skull. There it was. I knew it. The shell on my neck took my breath away.

I squeezed Ossibus's arm and pointed to the young woman. "There."

We both began to rush towards her. The old man must have seen us two pirates approach looking menacing and up to no good. He was feeble, hardly a threat, but he still tried to protect his child. "You can't have her. She is not for sale."

I took out from my leather satchel a bag of pearls and gems, our best. "No. She should never be for sale, and I would slaughter you if you tried to do that to her. I want that skull. Here is ample payment, but no questions and you are never to speak about us to anyone."

I placed the bag of jewels at her feet.

The young woman snatched the bag and lifted the skull to me. "It's yours. I had a dream a mermaid would take it from me. You're not a mermaid, but you could be."

"Thank you. Enjoy that loot."

Ossibus and I walked through the village with the very thing we had both been searching for. We were both put on that path but could not have completed it without each other. Before leaving the jetty to row back to the ship I stopped him. I had to. I'm not good at lying.

"Ossibus. Look at me."

He stopped.

I had to lift myself on my toes to kiss his lips, one of the best parts of his flesh left. I didn't need to peer into his eyes because the heat emanating from his skull told me everything I needed to know about how he felt. He grabbed me by the waist hard, pulling me close. His tongue played with mine. Finally, we had decided to come clean about whatever was developing between us. It was a kiss of lustful magic. The fishhooks on his face scraped my cheeks lightly but I didn't care. I would take his hook, flame, and flesh for as long as we had the will to sail.

"Sirena, is this a good idea? We are pirates with our own boats and crews sailing the seas alone. We have been in battle. What will everyone think about this sudden shift?"

"Since when did either of us give a toss about what anyone thought? That is why we have the respect of our crews."

"I guess you won't be in anyone else's bed but mine . . . haunt it and torment me as long as you want."

I kissed him one more time. "We should. But we need one more bit of insurance before we set our course for the king of Niaps."

"And that is?"

"Poison. The strongest venom I know of."

His lips curled to a smile. "Now that is the kind of pirate I love."

The guard appeared startled when he approached the king. "The . . . um, the queen . . . the previous one is here."

He bolted from his chair. "What? Did you scan her? Maybe it's a trap. How did she survive?"

"She says she wants to find favor with you again. Her family is willing to pay."

The king paused, looking at the large ruby set in steel on his little finger.

"Are you sure there is nothing on her that is a threat to me?"

"No weapons. Only organic materials she said were gifts from her time on the sea . . . an offering. One is a religious relic used by the nonbelievers. You can use it."

"Let her in. And go take a walk. She might not have been suitable to breed my heirs, but at least she was a good fuck."

The guard turned and walked out. He left the door open for Cassandra. She wore the white cotton blouse and indigo-dyed skirt. Worn brown leather boots padded quietly towards him. She smiled. "My king."

"Look at you. You made it back. I thought you would be dead. I guess you aren't as useless as I thought. Well, you can't stay. I have already taken another. You know how things work."

"I do. I also have information for you. You would be surprised at the people who inhabit the world beyond this island. The things I have seen."

The king shuffled backwards as Cassandra moved towards him. The skull felt heavy in her hand. She had an urge to let it go. It wasn't meant to be used, ever. Her fingers tingled. When his back was against the stone wall, she dropped the Skull of Wrath on the hard marble ground. It shattered with a loud cracking noise filling the room.

"What was that? Did you just break a gift for me?"

She flexed her hand and looked at the red cloth bag. "No, my love. I still have your gift."

Cassandra took out the sea urchin from her pocket and unwrapped it from a rough cotton cloth.

His eyes searched it with mild disgust as he brought his hand to his nose. "What is this? It hardly seems fit for a king."

Without warning Cassandra flipped her hand and smashed the sea urchin into his neck. The thick needles pierced his flesh, releasing streams of blood across Cassandra's face and shirt. He clutched his throat as his eyes bulged from the sockets. White foam erupted from his nostrils and mouth. The thick orange creature inside the spiny shell crawled out of the shell and slipped into his open mouth. It would feast until he was dead from the poison of the sea. And his court would feed on each other as they fought for power. This would give each territory enough time to rebel.

Cassandra knew she had to leave. Ossibus and Sirena waited at the port in the guise of trading merchants. She took the steel and ruby ring off the king's little finger before slipping through a door hidden behind a tapestry. It was steel and what was known as electronic. The ring was the key.

She rushed down the staircase and disappeared into the street. The sense of freedom overwhelmed her. She had everything she needed. The sea breeze picked up and lifted her hair from her shoulders. The elation of the king's death made her wish her hair could turn to feathers so she could fly off. But for now the open water would have to do until she found the place she wanted to set roots. Perhaps that day would never come. But it was nice to know she had the choice. From the distance she could see Ossibus and Sirena attempting to blend in and appear calm. They were far from being merchants as they were not trying to haggle or sell any apples from the large basket they had stolen from the fortress kitchen.

"Is it done?" I asked.

"The skull fell from my hand and shattered," Cassandra said. "It wanted that. I used the urchin."

Ossibus reached for my hand. "Where to next, Captain?"

I looked to Cassandra. "You want us to take you to your homeland?"

"No, maybe later. I want to see the world. Is it okay if I work on the ship with you?"

I nodded. "We might head into war depending on the fallout from this, but whatever comes next, we are free."

PALM BEACH POISON

Part 1: The Call

I held my smile, made it shine like a tiara glinting in the sunlight as I placed the platters of Nobu sushi on the table. At forty I had become good at keeping up appearances. It was a skill I learned growing up as a pageant kid in Texas. "Miss Congeniality. You want to win Miss Congeniality," my mother would say. Charisma and an easy-going smile had the power to make your skin appear a shade lighter and the frayed edges of any handsewn seam softer. Brown girls with attitude are trouble. Cholas. But rich white people aren't the only ones who can play the appearance game. I could feel my heart rate increase to banda music tempo as I held my tongue and fist knowing what my new employers had done and continued to do. If only there was enough mercury in the fatty tuna sashimi to poison them on the spot.

They chose khaki shorts to the knee so tight they gave me camel toe. These were paired with a pink polo equally as tight. My uniform. When I mentioned I needed a bigger size, they both frowned and said it was a perfect fit. No other sizes available anyway. I smiled and said it would work just fine. By the artwork strewn around the mansion, I should not have been surprised they wanted the female help to have every curve and cranny on show.

Three hundred dollars, not much more than their sushi. That is all that they felt the dignity and innocence of those girls were worth. Most of them the most vulnerable in our community, like my daughter Sophia's friend Crystal. That is why, despite not being a domestic worker, I took up work as a housekeeper for this socialite couple living in one of the most otherworldly places—Palm Beach. I was in my second year of law school doing the best I could later in life. With steady alimony, a loan, and two jobs, it was enough. Yes, we lived on the west side and didn't have a view, but we worked hard. We have no other choice. When things were tight, my mother also told me, "sink or swim." It's never too late to take up a new occupation, including murder and revenge.

You know what? Fuck that. Some of them across the bridge, like the one who owns Mar-a-Loco, are the very reason decent folks like us are left holding the motherfucking pails in a sinking boat. Who knows how many of *those* made their money looting the pockets of honest people or finding ways to avoid taxes on islands that used to be colonies. Still stolen money in a nation founded on stolen property and built by stolen people and fed by people whose children had their dreams stolen from them by La Migra. I had to do this. I had to find a way to stop the abuse. Law enforcement had shown they could be bought as easily as a drive-through meal deal.

My sixteen-year-old daughter knew she could trust me, despite the dirty looks we gave each other whenever we disagreed. We burned in our inability to understand each other's perspective and sometimes wouldn't talk for a full day, like the night I told her she couldn't go to a party at someone's house I didn't know. She stomped off as I expected, and I knew we would talk the next day. All my sternness fled when I received a call from the police a week later. I remember vividly the terse tone of the officer's voice requesting I come to a meeting at the school. "Can you please tell me what this is about?" I pleaded.

"I'm sorry, but this involves a minor. We need you to identify photos."

I rushed to the school shaking behind the wheel, the worst-case scenario razor-blading through my mind. The heat of the leather seats cut into my thighs as I tried to watch my speed, adding to my agitation. I arrived at 2 p.m. Sophia would still be in classes. I walked into the assigned empty classroom where two plainclothes detectives were waiting.

"Ms. Dominguez?"

I didn't smile or say hello. I sat down and squeezed my handbag. I wondered why the school and not the police station.

"I'm Detective Renada and this is Detective Maddox. We are from the Palm Beach unit. We have been alerted to young girls at this school attending parties and that some of them had photos taken of them. We need to formally identify them all."

Detective Renada was a woman with streaks of gray hair pulled back into a ponytail. She looked slightly older than me and possibly a mother with the way her mouth was closed tightly and brows furrowed while she studied my face. Whatever this was deeply bothered her. She slowly pushed the photo towards me across the table. "Do you recognize the clothing or any other identifiable marks on this child?"

Her companion, Detective Maddox, a man in his fifties, looked slightly bored. I didn't want to look, but I had to. My eyes scanned the photo. I didn't recognize the half-clothed body. Just looking at it sent a chill the length of both arms. I shook my head and turned away. *My baby. My baby. What happened to MY baby?* My thoughts twisted to scenarios I tried to dismiss, but flashes of horror made me shake in my seat.

"Are you sure? How about this one?"

Detective Maddox pulled another photo from a manila folder on the top of a towering stack and slid it in front of me. I sucked in air and then bit my lip. I recognized the dark brown mole the size of the head of a thumbtack, but it wasn't my daughter's neck. It belonged to Crystal. She hated it. That lip color looked like the shade my daughter had pestered me to borrow until I gave it to her even though it was Chanel and expensive. A treat I bought for my interviews. It makes your mouth look like a fuchsia bougainvillea bloom. When you are young all you want is to be older, dress older, have adult experiences. Then when you're my age, all those regrets and lost moments of youth haunt you. I regretted allowing her to wear my lipstick, but when I was her age I experimented with my mother's and auntie's makeup.

"I believe that to be my daughter's friend, Crystal Derry. She lives with her grandmother. Why am I here and not her grandmother?"

Detective Renada folded her hands on the table. "Thank you. When you leave, a teacher will take you to your daughter and Crystal."

No fucking way I was moving. I looked at them in quick succession and placed my bag on the table. "What happened? What is this about?"

Detective Renada remained silent yet met my eyes. She knew I would cause a fuss because that was what she would do. "It's an ongoing investigation, but it looks like girls were being paid to model designer clothes. Photos and videos were taken of them without their knowledge as they undressed. Some were paid to massage an older gentleman. We just needed an identification, but we couldn't reach an adult for Ms. Derry. She said to contact you."

I was relieved and then immediately hated myself for feeling that way. Crystal was a good kid from bad circumstances. Like so many others, her immediate family was caught in the opioid crisis. She'd told me snippets about her mother who I met once at a barbeque. From what Crystal told me, her mother was in and out of jail or bouncing house to house with different boyfriends. Crystal did what she could for her younger brother, but he eventually was taken into foster care for missing too much school. The grandmother didn't feel she could care for a seven-year-old. Crystal came and went as she pleased.

"May I have your cards, detectives?" They looked at each other before rummaging through pockets. I scanned the stack of folders trying to count how many were there. Too many to count. I wanted to puke.

I walked to the door of the classroom, not knowing what I would say to my daughter. My mind and belly were a mixture of revulsion, anger, and fear. Then I wanted to know who did this? Where could I find them? I could feel my temper rising the longer I walked next to the teacher, who avoided looking at or talking to me. Walking into the principal's office took me back to when I was a teen and the one time I was called in for ditching two weeks before graduating high school. But the revulsion and anger came from the first time my mother had told me *her* story.

Crystal and Sophia both appeared red-eyed with their makeup smeared. Sophia gave me the same look she had since she was four and had done something wrong. All I wanted to do was scoop her into my arms and tell her it was all right. I would make it better and make it go away, like I did when we checked beneath her bed and in the closets every night until she was nine. "Come on girls. In the car."

We left the school in silence and didn't speak until we arrived home. I went straight to the kitchen and got us all drinks from the fridge before sitting at the dining table. In that moment I truly felt my age, feeling like my own mother always looked when we "needed to talk."

'I'm not mad. I just want to know what happened."

Sophia and Crystal stared at their fizzing sodas; the only sound in the entire house was the sound of ice cracking.

Crystal broke down first. "I'm sorry Mrs. D. I didn't mean to get Sophia into trouble. I was told if I brought a friend to a party, I could earn money . . ."

"Crystal, it's okay. But what happened to you is not, and it is not your fault. They're fucking adults taking advantage. Fucking pig motherfuckers . . ." My voice took a volume all its own, louder, and I had to stop by the look on their faces as I cursed and spit. A woman possessed by righteous rage, blinding me. I composed myself. I composed myself like I had when my mother told me her secret. It made sense why she was so overprotective. Why she wanted me to shine and be somebody even if it was based on something as superficial as beauty. But I promised her if I ever saw the family-member-predator who crept into her bedroom, I would out him as a pedophile pig in front of everyone before spitting in his face.

"Just start from the beginning. Don't leave a single detail out, even if you didn't tell it to the police. I need to know. You can trust me. I will keep you safe." I meant every word. I steeled myself for the truth of what happened at the party. Crystal spoke first.

Part 2: The Party

"This thing is in Palm Beach? Who the hell you know there?" Sophia quickly packed her favorite lipstick and tube top to change into in the car. Crystal didn't know what to say, really. She had been there once to give the guy a massage and model clothes for his girlfriend, Giselle Wells, some rich bitch from England. The massage made her feel gross and awkward, his skin pulling away from his frame as she touched his body. He'd turned around on the massage table, exposing his erection through the towel. Before she could react, he'd grabbed her hands and placed them on his chest. "Why did you stop? Nothing you haven't seen before, I'm sure." It wasn't, and those memories hurt. Hurt worse than when she gave herself a second ear piercing. She continued to massage his chest and when he slipped his hand beneath the towel, Crystal floated far away and focused on the money next to the bathtub.

Before she left, she was told about a party with other girls. "Bring friends. I have a ton of new sunglasses straight from the designers themselves," the British woman said with a large smile and hand on her shoulder. Crystal was skeptical, but no one seemed forced to do anything. They could leave with the money before anything bad happened. There would be safety in a group. An older girl, Jenny, who first brought her to the Palm Beach property, would be picking them up.

Sophia couldn't find Crystal. The party seemed like a few girls drinking alcohol and gossiping with each other. Sometimes an older woman moved through the crowd with handfuls of designer clothes and accessories draped over her arm while the girls took photos for Instagram and TikTok. Sophia didn't know why, but that woman with the pixie cut, black hair, and British accent made her feel uncomfortable, like her brown eyes should be black because something dark dwelled there. For all her money, this woman dressed pretty frumpy and appeared plain as hell. Sophia made her way around with a lukewarm orange juice with vodka. The house was huge, white, and with high ceilings. They obviously had no children or pets. It was decorated like a museum dedicated to the bodies of young women. Busts, statues, photographs, and paintings like a gallery dedicated to sex. Sophia continued to wander. Perhaps Crystal was in the bathroom or smoking a joint. That's when she saw the door to a bathroom ajar and her best friend's chin touching her chest. Tears fell from Crystal's cheeks as she buttoned her blouse. An older man stepped out of the shower with his gray chest hair and pubes, and a smirk that made her feel like she stood in an outdoor toilet, but that is what men like that think of women. Toilets. That's what men like that think of people, as disposable as a used condom.

Sophia ran back to the party and would wait until Crystal walked to the main room. Every laugh and shout made Sophia jump. The music gave her vertigo. What the hell was this party? After what seemed like hours but was more like ten minutes, Crystal rejoined the group. Sophia wasted no time grabbing her friend's hand. "We have to leave. I don't like this. I don't feel well."

Crystal looked like she had refreshed her makeup, her eyeliner dark on the bottom lid. "But we don't have a ride home. Jenny left."

"I don't care. Let's go outside at least and figure it out."

"All right. I guess." Crystal followed.

The humidity of the night and mosquitoes attacked them immediately. Cicadas chirped loudly. The alcohol surged in their blood. Sophia spotted a Mexican man wiping down a black escalade in the last of the light at 8:30 p.m. He looked a little older than her father. "Hey, can we get a ride please? Just across the bridge. I'm Sophia and this is Crystal."

"Arturo." He looked at these girls; girls, not women. He hated seeing them here, but the pay was excellent.

"I'm not supposed to leave. You all right?"

Sophia's heart sped. At the very last resort she would call her mom and be grounded for the rest of her life. "No. There is an emergency at home. Please. I'm begging you. Just across the bridge."

Arturo glanced towards the white mansion, a mansion of secrets and sin. "Just this once. Don't tell anyone."

Part 3: The Plan

I didn't sleep that night. I listened to the air conditioning and toyed with the idea of just getting out of bed to drink wine alone. Both girls had broken down, crying hysterically as they shared the details of what had happened to Crystal and what my daughter saw. The reality of being a woman brought upon them before their time. What a fucked up, warped reality some of us live in every day. I thought of all the times I had been grabbed. Cocks shown to me and stroked before my eyes without permission. Nearly jumped out of a bus one of those times into stopped traffic when I looked down to see a man stroking himself in his car next to my bus full of school kids. I remembered the time after a first date. Something about him felt off so I called it a night after two drinks. My instinct was validated when I had to physically push him away with all my strength and charm before squeezing behind my door. All with a smile on my face as I laughed off his insistence. I stood at that locked door, scared for my body as he begged to be let in. He stood there for half an hour telling me to let him in. No sleep that night hoping he wouldn't break into my shitty apartment. Never did I think my child would experience that. Not my daughter. We would evolve from it. And here we were. But I had faith justice would be served for the girls in the photographs. The detectives had a stack of proof, plus Crystal's testimony and who knows how many others. I waited for the system to work it out.

Ill placed faith. The door that had kept a potential predator out of my apartment was stronger. The predator's lawyer, a famous white man teaching at a famous law school about a constitution that does harm as it does good, helped Jerry and Giselle to go free. When a warrant was finally given to search his property, it was clean. No computers, no cameras. Nothing. *He knew.* Someone had told him there would be a search of his property.

Another sleepless night wanting to drink to oblivion in order to sleep. I couldn't focus on the work I had to do over the summer. The summer. All these girls with nowhere to go or anything to do and in need of money. *Summer.* I began to hatch my plan. These assholes had a type. They were like daisies, young white girls or light-skinned Latinas. They bruise easily to the touch because most of them are already bruised by someone else. Unlike roses, daisies aren't prized. But there are Black daisies and Brown daisies. There are daises all over the world being preyed upon in any given second and the lower they are on the socioeconomic ladder, the easier it is to strip them of their petals. Jerry Epping was just one. One I could stop. When the clock turned to 5 a.m. I jumped out of bed to begin my plan with methodical precision.

First, I needed the girls safe. That would be easy for Sophia because she was due to go on a road trip with her father to Niagara Falls. I managed to get ahold of Crystal's grandmother. She didn't care one way or another what her granddaughter did for the summer. I didn't bother asking for money either because I didn't want it to be an issue. The outcome would be priceless, like the girls themselves.

"All summer." Sophia cocked her head and crossed her arms.

"Yes, all summer."

"Mom. Grace is tight with the snacks and we have to write book reports on the drive. And no phones at night."

"Good. It will be a fun vacation. And I like Grace. I'm glad your father is happy."

"Mrs. D are you sure I'm welcome?" Crystal watched helplessly, still not knowing where she belonged in all of this mess.

"Crystal, you are always welcome to stay with us and share whatever we have. Next school year I'm happy for you to live with us if you want. I just think it's best you all get out of town and away. You guys are gonna do all that fun camping stuff. Hiking. Stop at different beaches and lakes."

A large grin spread across Crystal's face. "Sophia, you didn't tell me camping. Can we do s'mores every night?"

"See, Crystal is excited. It will be fun."

Of course, my child had to roll her eyes just like her mama and flick her hoop earrings when she tossed her hair to the side. "When do we leave?"

It pained me to my core to know I wouldn't see my child for months. I was pissed at the cops for doing fuck all and at Jerry for his pedophilic ways. "You leave the day after school ends."

Phase two. I knew I couldn't just roll up to this guy's house and ask for a job and I'm sure he wasn't advertising on Gumtree.

"Detective Renada. Hello again. It's been a few weeks, I think?" The detective had to be tired of me because since our first meeting I'd called regularly for an update. I nagged and burrowed like a tick out for blood. But since I was not Crystal's parent, they couldn't tell me shit.

"Hello, Mrs. Dominguez. I have no information. The case is done. Been watching the news?"

"I just want to talk. Look, the biggest problem is evidence, right? Someone tipped them off and everything that could have been used as evidence taken? Their staff didn't want to talk either."

She remained silent but didn't hang up, so I pressed on. "Get me a job with them. Maybe I can be an informant."

She let out an exhausted heavy sigh before answering. "There was only one guy in the house who was remotely friendly. His name is Arturo. I'll see what I can do. Don't get your hopes up and no promises."

A week later I began my job as a housekeeper after sending a short résumé and full-body photograph. Arturo opened the gate for me when I arrived at the mansion.

"Hey, I'm Arturo. Welcome," said a man who could have easily been my uncle. He seemed like a nice guy, but appearances don't mean shit. Jerry made his fortune on appearances and lies.

"You do the driving?"

"Yeah, and whatever else they might need doing here and there. You know, you look familiar."

"Well, I am Mexican and as they say, we are all the same."

Arturo chuckled cheerfully. "Yep, don't I know it. I'm supposed to show you around. By the way, if anyone asks you are a friend who fell on hard times and needed a job. Jerry likes to offer things to be helpful. Finally took him up on his goodwill and got you a job. This is as far as I get involved."

Phase three. I needed to scrub the house. Scrub with my eyes, brain, and ears. The movement of the staff. The routines of Jerry and Giselle. I memorized every step until

I got home and could write it all down in a notebook. Every morning I called my daughter to check in and tell her I loved her. After, I cried into my coffee at the silly things that annoyed her. Silly things I would miss. But young women are worth more than all Jerry's Swiss watches left in a safe.

My plan didn't have a direction for a month. Just observing. And then I met Jerry for the second time as I made pico de gallo and salsa. I could feel his presence before I could see him. He was used to being a big deal, demanding attention and praise. He carried himself with the arrogant swagger of invincible royalty, an invisible authority on his head like a crown. Every jewel is an accomplishment even if they were procured by lying and cheating. Raping. Raping the system and raping bodies. How many Black and Brown men in super max for less. He stood next to me, not saying anything, just watching me finely chop cilantro, and then finally at me directly. His eyes roving every inch, inspecting every wrinkle and curve. But at my age he knew I had my fair share of men and cocks. I'm a younger man's fantasy Men like this want something new to mold, to train. "So, you are the one who makes that delicious stuff? Found it in the fridge the other day. Really good."

Remember to be Miss Congeniality even though you are the only brown contestant in a handstitched dress.

"Thank you. It was a recipe I learned from my aunt."

"You have daughters?"

I continued to dice the tomatoes, thinking of the sharpness of the knife. "No. Sons."

Jerry grabbed a slice of red pepper off the chopping board. He felt too close to me. "I bet they're good-looking boys. Probably get a lot of pussy. I can't imagine how pretty your daughters would be. You probably looked good in your twenties."

"I don't know, sir. Long time ago."

"Let me know if I can help them with a job or college. I have friends who can mentor them. They like to help boys from underprivileged backgrounds. Money is no issue for you or your boys if you need assistance."

My stomach dropped faster than kids in front of a broken piñata. The sick fuck really thought I couldn't see through his fake compassion, his greasy smile slathered thick while his eyes were black coals.

"They don't live with me. They're with their father."

He eased off. "Oh. I see. Hey, love the food. Maybe you can make me and Giselle dinner some time." He walked away. I thanked God both Sophia and Crystal were far from here. I drove home screaming to "Hotel California" by the Eagles because it reminded me of sitting in the car next to my mother. She always sang to The Eagles. I kept repeating, "You can never leave." I thought how people like him might be stabbed a million times, but you could never kill the beast. The beast of class and race. The beast of patriarchy. "Hotel California" was released when my mother was around the same age as my daughter. She had me only a few years later.

I stayed up nights scouring for information to back up the rumors about Jerry and the people he befriended. These pass-around parties. The trafficking. A plan was beginning to form. Then Jerry and Giselle left for a week to his private island. I would have one week to work out the details of how this would end. To get my affairs in order.

Giselle Wells popped pills. She kept them in the bathroom cabinet and I often picked them up for her from the pharmacy. I used my stone molcajete given to me by my grandfather on one of his trips to Mexico to grind two bottles of muscle relaxants to the size of jalapeno seeds for the best damn batch of salsa I had ever fucking made. I knew they would return from the island tired and want to eat. It was perfect. But they surprised me with a girl in tow. Fuck. I would stick to the plan. They wanted to eat outside. I placed the bowl of ancho chili muscle-relaxant salsa on a tray with chips from the best Mexican restaurant in west Palm Beach. In a small vase, a few daisies. A bottle of Montrachet white wine and two glasses.

"Looks amazing. Can I get some?"

I whipped my head towards the girl they had with them. "No. It's not for you."

She frowned. "But . . ."

I grabbed her arm hard, hard like a mother pulling her running child about to step foot into oncoming traffic. I looked her in the eye. "I said no. Leave. Please, go. This is not for you. Do you understand?"

Her eyes quivered with tears. "I'll stay in my room tonight."

"Good." She walked away into some cavern in that house. I looked at the platter one last time before walking out to the terrace by the pool. So much for my law career.

Aftermath

When I saw their bodies blue lipped and cold on their bed, I felt satisfaction. A service to the world had been done. After finishing the salsa and wine, both felt unwell and retired to their room. They never woke up. It was a small hearing and execution because the system designed to serve and protect only did so for those who could afford it. Both of these people had escaped justice. No longer. Some might say I have taken away their day in court. There would be more court days. For all the others complicit. For all the others who used their services. I called Detective Renada. All their computers, iPad, phones, and electronics were still in the house. No one to tip them off because they were dead. I couldn't cover up what I did. I couldn't blame it on anyone else. But I had a story.

"This just in. A forty-year-old mother of one has been arrested for the double homicide of Jerry Epping and Giselle Wells. She claims she had been in a state of extreme distress and temporarily insane after seeing photos Mr. Epping was previously accused of taking of underage girls. She says she has proof of his alleged crimes and that no one else helped her in any way in the double homicide. Her daughter has begun an online campaign to free her mother including a GoFundMe for her legal expenses. This is a story we will continue to cover."

I sat across from my lawyer, Alex Dersch, the famous constitutional law attorney who got Jerry and Giselle off before. He also happened to be a close friend to Jerry. Enough money was raised in a GoFundMe to pay for his services. I didn't want any other lawyer but him. A test.

"So, Alex, it doesn't bother you that I murdered your swindling, lying, pedophile friend?"

He didn't smile. I could see the venom in his eyes. I was surprised when he took me on as a client. Probably so he wouldn't be accused of wrongdoing like before. But these motherfuckers and their egos. Yeah, possession is a real phenomenon. He still maintained his innocence. I'm sure he had some fucked-up definition of innocence he twisted for himself. "I'm a defense attorney. You hired me, and it's an interesting case. When have I ever not defended controversial people? My question is why did you choose me?

I leaned in close, ready to give my victory speech after a sash is placed over you and a crown on your head. "Because I want you to get me, a brown woman with few means out of this. You have done it for people like yourself. Now do it for me. Take the fucking money. Make yourself even more famous and free me. I want to be a lawyer like you someday. Make it happen."

He didn't flinch and neither did I.

"Okay. I will get to work."

Yes, I am a double murderer, and if there is a God, then I will answer to him when I'm dead, and if he is like all the ones down here, then I will poison him, too.

V. CASTRO is a Mexican American writer from San Antonio, Texas now residing in the UK with her family. She writes Latinx narratives in horror, erotic horror, and science fiction. Her recent releases include *Aliens: Vasquez* and *Goddess of Filth*.

Creature Publishing was founded on a passion for feminist discourse and horror's potential for social commentary and catharsis. Seeking to address the gender imbalance and lack of diversity traditionally found in the horror genre, Creature is a platform for stories which challenge the status quo. Our definition of feminist horror, broad and inclusive, expands the scope of what horror can be and who can make it.

www.ingramcontent.com/pod-product-compliance
Ingram Content Group UK Ltd.
Pitfield, Milton Keynes, MK11 3LW, UK
UKHW042112090525
458401UK00002B/7